ATTACK!

Suddenly Dwight saw the wolves.

One moment there was nothing. The next, there were those two lean, gray shapes gliding silently over the snow. . . .

The she-wolf went off to one side. Her mate sprang to meet the big mutt. They closed in mid-air. The she-wolf came in below them, slashing up from the side.

The big dog made no sound as they struck him. There was something grim and chilling about the terrible silence of those first few split seconds after the dog and he-wolf met, jaw to jaw. . . .

Critics' Corner:

"A gripping, realistic picture of the North Dakota Badlands in a time of bitter cold and blizzard when wolves prey on sheep. Big Mutt, an abandoned dog, must kill to live but eventually proves his value as a sheepdog and justifies a young boy's supreme faith in him."
—Library Journal

"Without being in the least sentimental, it has both drama and pathos. Big Mutt is an exceptionally good dog character."
—Saturday Review

"The dog's fight to live and the boy's efforts to save and reclaim him are told with gripping suspense and realism."
—A.L.A. Booklist

"...this realistic story of a boy, of dogs and sheep and wolves has some unforgettable scenes....There are graphic details of the posse's search for Big Mutt, of a lambing season, and, throughout, of the intensity of conflict and devotion between animals and men."
—Horn Book

Other Recommendations: A.L.A. Basic Book Collection for Elementary Grades; National Council of Teachers of English; H. W. Wilson Children's Catalog; H. W. Wilson Junior High School Library Catalog; a Junior Literary Guild selection; *New York Herald Tribune* Honor Book, 1952.

About the Author:

JOHN REESE, the eldest of six children, was born in Western Nebraska and graduated from Dunbar (Nebraska) High School. For many years he was a reporter for the *Los Angeles Examiner,* which he left in 1948 to start a career in free-lancing. He has written magazine articles and stories, as well as books for young readers. Mr. Reese now lives in East Hartford, Connecticut. He is married with three children, and his hobbies include photography and jazz music.

BIG
MUTT

by John Reese

Illustrated by ROD RUTH

AN ARCHWAY PAPERBACK
POCKET BOOKS · NEW YORK

BIG MUTT

Archway Paperback edition published November, 1969
6th printing .... September, 1977

Published by
POCKET BOOKS, a Simon & Schuster Division of
GULF & WESTERN CORPORATION
1230 Avenue of the Americas, New York, N.Y. 10020.

Archway Paperback editions are distributed in the U.S. by
Simon & Schuster, Inc., 1230 Avenue of the Americas,
New York, N.Y. 10020, and in Canada by Simon & Schuster
of Canada, Ltd., Richmond Hill, Ontario, Canada.

ISBN: 0-671-29872-0.
Printed in the U.S.A.

For
Marylou, Catherine, and Andrew,
and their friends

BIG MUTT

By John Reese

Illustrated by Rod Ruth

CHAPTER ONE

THE BIG DOG FILLED THE REAR SEAT OF THE car. He was too big for any car, and this was a small one, heavily loaded with suitcases and boxes and baskets and folded blankets. He did not look comfortable, with his ungainly legs doubled under him, but he did look as though he knew how to make the best of things.

He was a huge dog. He would stand thirty-two inches at the shoulder, with a weight of one hundred and thirty pounds. Much of this was fat, but no amount of fat could hide the immense strength of his powerful legs and back. His ears seemed too small for such a heavy head and wide jaw. They were almost hound ears, except that at odd sounds he shot them forward in his sleep, as no hound could do.

He was not a handsome dog. His size, and the brindle coloring over most of his body, proved great Dane blood. He was neither long-haired nor short-haired, but somewhere in between. This shagginess, which went to wolf gray on his back, showed Alsatian or German shepherd blood. And

1

there was probably also some mastiff, and some that was just plain dog.

No, he was not handsome. He was just a mutt, a mongrel with a head as big as a gallon jug, and feet that would make tracks the size of a small saucer.

The driver of the car was a middle-aged man. Beside him sat his wife, knitting. The radio droned music. The car heater hummed steadily, for this was North Dakota, in January. There was old snow on the ground, dirty and hard-packed, and the wind blowing steadily down from Canada had an icy dampness.

The woman looked up from her knitting. "I keep feeling a draft on my neck," she said.

"Of course you do," her husband grumbled. "That dog has jammed one of the windows open. Look at him!"

The dog opened one eye and then promptly went back to sleep. He had pushed and pushed with his big nose until he had sprung one of the little vent glasses open. Now it could not be closed at all. The dog lay with his nose against this crack, to catch the sharply cold air that hissed past.

There was nothing to interest him in this wild, empty country. He was a city dog, born in a New York alley, raised on New York streets until the woman had found him. Cars and buses, traffic and people—these he knew, especially people. But the faint, wild scents that came now meant nothing to him.

2

The car sped on, hour after hour, heading into the sinking sun, which showed itself redly under a black dome of thick clouds. It passed a herd of cattle feeding at cribs beside the road. The dog's nose wrinkled slightly. His great Dane ancestors had been fierce boar-hunting dogs in the forests of early Germany, and he had inherited their keen hunting nose. But he had never used it, and the faint cow smell was quickly gone, leaving the lazy dog unstirred.

Stronger than the cow smell, and more frequently met, was the scent of sheep. This country was too rough for cattle, and was not even very good sheep range. At this season, the sheep were penned close to the ranch houses, where they could be carefully watched, and fed and sheltered under long, low, open sheds. Not until the late Dakota spring made the slopes green would they be turned out to graze on the open hills.

Again and again the dog's nose wrinkled in his sleep as they passed these little roadside ranches. He was too lazy to wake up, but not too lazy to have strange, wild dreams.

But once something made him sit up suddenly, with a low, deep growl. The scent was quickly gone. He pressed his nose against the crack and snuffed loudly.

"I think he saw the cute little dog that ran across the road behind us," said the woman.

"What dog?" the man asked.

"That pretty little tan one with the bushy tail. It

looked like part Pomeranian, or part police dog. I wonder who it belongs to, so far from any house? Poor thing—it's probably lost."

It was neither a Pomeranian nor a police dog, although it did resemble both, with its bushy tail, fox-like face, and quick nimbleness. It was not a dog at all, but a coyote. The scent of this bold, smart, wild little second cousin of his had awakened the big mutt.

The man was a fast driver. They did not talk much. When they did, it was usually to quarrel.

The dog was used to this too. He had always known that the man disliked him and that the woman was his protector. They had always argued over him. What he did not know was that the man was determined to get rid of him before they returned to New York, and that his wife was gradually weakening. The man was weak, but the woman was weaker.

"I can't imagine anyone living here," the woman said.

"You don't have to," her husband grumbled. "This whole crazy trip was your idea. If you'd listened to me, we'd be taking it easy back in good old New York."

She began to cry. "It's my money. My own aunt left it to me. If I want to see the world, is that wrong?"

"Does that mutt have to see the world too? Look at him! He's ruining the car."

"Well, the car's mine too—don't forget that."

She looked back at the dog, sighing. "Poor Buster! Really, I didn't think he'd be such a nuisance."

"Buster! What a name for that monster!"

She cried harder. "How could I know such a darling little dog would grow up to be so big?"

All day they had bickered, because the woman had taken a wrong turn the night before, while the man slept. All-weather highways were few and far between here, and she had turned off on a narrow state road. They had gone nearly a hundred miles before her husband discovered her mistake.

It was then, while they had studied their maps in the cold, gray light of dawn, that the radio music faded and the announcer came on, to give a solemn storm warning.

They were Easterners—city people. They had no idea how terrible a winter storm could be here. But the clouds had been thickening heavily all day, and the bite of the wind had increased as the temperature dropped. Night seemed very close, yet there had been no twilight.

A few minutes ago they had stopped at a filling station in one of the small towns along the way. The old man who waited on them warned them to get back to the Federal highway as quickly as possible.

"Otherwise," he said, "we'll be out looking for you with a snowplow . . . and we may dig you out in time, and we may not. This is the last town for quite a stretch."

Now they were still trying to get back to the

highway, pushing the little car as hard as it would go.

This was the southern edge of the Badlands. North of the road, the snow lay in endless deep ridges and furrows as far as the eye could see. Where the snow had blown away, the soil showed a fierce, fiery red. For the most part there were no trees, no farmed fields, no houses or towns. In a few flat places there were hayfields, stubble fields, and small ranches; and shortly after leaving the last town, they had passed a small white school-house with a tall steeple. But these signs of life were few and far between.

The prairie dogs and gophers owned most of this raw, red country, and their only visitors were the coyotes and skunks who hunted them. The early French explorers had called this gullied land *"les terres mauvaises."* Later English-speaking set-tlers merely translated this name into their own language, and it became the Badlands.

Bad they were; and beyond them was Canada and its open prairie provinces, Manitoba and Sas-katchewan and Alberta. Up there was the Atha-basca country, the "Mother of Storms." Straight across Athabasca, down from the Arctic Circle, was this great storm moving on the heels of a strong north wind.

The car sped on toward the storm. Behind, somewhere, was the Little Missouri River, some-times little more than a wide creek, sometimes a roaring flood that covered thousands of square miles. Not far away were the Killdeer Mountains, not tall and lofty like America's great ranges, but high and cold and wild, and beautiful in a lonely way.

It was this loneliness that made the couple in the car fearful. The fat, lazy dog knew nothing of their fear, and cared less. He was two years old, and for a long time this couple had fed him and bathed him and exercised him and kept him out of trouble. So he slept, counting on them to take good care of him, no matter what happened.

The woman put down her knitting. "It's going to be pitch dark soon, and it's only four o'clock. I wish we'd reach a town. What if we did get snowbound? Is there any food in the car?"

"Some potato chips and a couple of cans of stuff," her husband said uneasily. "Say, was that sleet?"

It was sleet, a brief barrage that rattled loudly on the windshield. Suddenly the radio music stopped. The announcer's voice broke in:

"Your attention, please. We interrupt this program to bring you an important message. The storm predicted earlier today now appears to be moving southward more swiftly, and is expected to reach Montana and North Dakota early tonight. School authorities are warned to take every precaution to protect pupils today, and shippers of perishable freight should . . ."

The man snapped off the radio, as though

hoping he could shut off the storm at the same time.

"I'd feel better if we didn't have that dog along," he said. "He's just one more mouth to feed."

They passed a roadside sign:

DANGER!
Livestock Crossing—400 Ft.

No one had warned them that here livestock had the right-of-way over automobiles. They rounded a curve and the man stepped on the brake suddenly. A flock of sheep was crossing the road from south to north. The woman's eyes grew wide with amazement as the milling sea of bleating, hurrying creatures parted around the car and flowed on. Two woolly, black-and-white dogs raced up and down beside the sheep, barking shrilly, nagging them to hurry.

The big mutt in the back seat of the car sat up and cocked his houndlike ears. His big nose wrinkled at the strange, pungent scent that filled the air.

"Look—there's a man with them!" the woman cried, as the last of the sheep passed the car and streamed up the north slope, and her husband prepared to start the car.

"Just a kid," the man said disappointedly. "But maybe he can tell us where we are."

"The kid" was a short, sturdy boy of about

fifteen, heavily muffled against the cold. He wore high leather boots with wool socks turned down over them, a wool scarf, and a wool Scotch cap that covered his ears with fur flaps. Under his sheepskin-lined Mackinaw he had a sweater, a vest, and two shirts. Yet for all this weight of clothing he did not seem clumsy.

The man blew the horn. The boy came to the side of the car, covering his face against the bite of the sleet that suddenly peppered him. When he took his mittened hands away, they saw big, dark eyes in a serious, good-looking, freckled face. The eyes grew bigger still as the big mutt leaned forward on the stack of baggage and thumped his heavy tail.

"Jeepers, what a dog!"

"How far to the highway, sonny?" the man asked.

"About twenty miles." The boy had to shout to be heard over the storm. "Just stay on this road and turn south when it turns. Say, that's some dog. What kind is he?"

"Half great Dane and half appetite, I think. Straight ahead, you say?"

"Yes, sir. You can't miss it. I've got an Irish wolfhound, sir. I thought they were the biggest dogs in the world, but he's bigger than Colleen. What do you call him?"

"It doesn't matter, just so you don't call him too late for supper. Speaking of names, what's yours?"

"Dwight Jerome, sir."

"Live around here?"

"About a mile north of here, sir."

"O.K., Dwight. Catch!"

The man flipped a dime to the boy, and drove on.

After a while he said: "We don't seem to be getting anywhere. Seems like we've gone twenty miles since we saw those sheep. I wish I'd kept track on the speedometer."

The woman began to cry again. "I'm afraid. I wish we had some food. What if we had to stay in the car for days, like those people in the newsreels?"

The man did not answer. His own fear was as great as hers, but he tried not to show it.

The wind rose as they topped a little grade, rocking their car violently. Then the road went down into a deep cut and turned a curve, and the wind was shut off. The man stopped the car and turned to his wife, not quite meeting her eyes.

"We can't get any more food," he said, "but we can get rid of one eater. We'd better get rid of that dog before we go any farther."

"Dump Buster out?" the woman wailed. "Oh, no!"

"We'll all starve if we don't," the man argued. "If we turn him loose he'll make out. There must be lots of rabbits and wild animals here."

"Oh, I couldn't stand to dump Buster out!"

"Maybe you'd rather starve yourself," he said angrily.

"No. Oh, I don't know what to do!"

"Make up your mind! I tell you, it's the kindest thing. Listen to that wind."

It was not the kindest thing to dump a soft, spoiled, city-raised dog out in this lean sheep country, in the worst blizzard the Northwest had known in a generation.

But they did it. The man opened the car door and said, "Out, Buster!"

The dog got out gladly. For a long time he had been wanting to stretch his long legs. He went bounding awkwardly up the grade to where the strong wind caught him. It felt good, after the close confinement of the car.

For a minute, that is. When he grew cold and turned to start back, the car was just vanishing up the far grade into the storm.

The dog did not worry. His people had gone off and left him before, and they always came back. He sat down beside the road to wait for them. But the tire tracks filled swiftly with snow, and they did not return.

He whined. He was hungry, and it was time for the woman to open some cans of dog food and put it in the little bowl they carried in the back of the car. He got up restlessly and hunted for a more sheltered place. Here he lay down. Night came, and he still waited, but not a single car came along the narrow, lonely road.

By now, the man and woman had already reached the Federal highway. A few more miles and they came to a small town, where there were a motel and a restaurant, and a place to store the car until this blizzard was over. They were quite gay as they put the car away and tramped through the storm on their way to supper.

"I wonder where Buster is now?" the woman sighed as they ate.

"Probably having a high old time," the man said. "Say, he'll get a big kick out of catching rabbits. A dog likes that kind of life, you know."

It made him feel better to pretend he had done a kind thing. Now that his stomach was full, he thought guiltily of the dog's empty one. Now that he was warm, his conscience nagged him because the dog might be cold. His wife was fond of the dog and would make him miserable if she thought the dog was in trouble.

"It was the kindest thing we could have done," he said again.

CHAPTER TWO

THE DOG'S THICK LAYER OF FAT would keep him from starving for a while. It would also furnish some protection for his vital organs, insulating his blood stream against the killing cold. But he needed shelter. To lie too long in this rapidly dropping temperature meant quick death.

He thought he needed food worse, though, because this was his usual supper time. He had never hunted before. The hunting strain was almost, but not quite, dead in him. Besides a hunter's keen nose, he had a hunter's powerful jaws, its killing strength and overwhelming weight. He was soft and fat, but the framework of a meat eater who could hunt his own food was there, under the fat.

Instinct made him trot back up the road toward where he had seen the sheep. Their scent was now smothered in snow. He tried, lonesomely, to track them a little way, remembering the boy more than the sheep, turning to humans in his time of need.

But the broad trail was blotted out, the flock gone. Lost, he stopped and turned his heavy head into the wind, seeking the scents that meant people and food and warmth.

None came. He stood there a moment, snuffing and whining, shaking himself from time to time to dislodge the snow that piled on him.

It was the cold that moved him finally. He tucked his tail between his legs and let the wind push him along. He floundered through the growing drifts and fell into snow-filled gullies he could not see, not knowing when he wandered off the road. The snow quickly covered his huge tracks.

At last the wind stopped buffeting him, and he found himself in a deep gully, the banks of which offered some protection. But not much. On and on he floundered, the gully growing deeper and deeper. Suddenly a deep hole yawned blackly in front of him. He yelped in terror as his forefeet slid over the edge. His powerful hind feet clawed wildly for footing.

He fell almost twenty feet, reaching the bottom with no more than a few small bruises. Here the snow had fallen evenly, unstirred by wind. He picked himself up, turned, and growled deep in his throat as a strange, wild scent came to him from only a few feet away.

Water from countless tearing floods had cut this deep gully. The whole area was a network of gullies, making it worthless for grazing. Here, numerous families of coyotes had made their dens. It was the scent of one of these that came sharply to the big mutt's nostrils.

It was a lucky find for him, because the old male that was head of this family of five coyotes had hidden their den skillfully. The coyotes heard the big mutt crashing through the deep snow, and scurried out into the storm, rather than fight him. They had worn a little winding path up the steep wall. They fled in single file, snarling silently, the old he-coyote in the lead.

The dog let them go and crawled into their warm cave, which they had padded with grass and the roots of grass. A badger had first built this home, and the coyotes had driven him out and enlarged it to suit their needs. It was low down in the side of the gully, well-hidden, protected from the wind, yet high enough so that not even the deepest spring floodwaters would enter.

The dog lay down contentedly in his warm bed. He groaned and scratched and stretched, and his New York license tag tinkled against the small brass plate on his collar, which said:

OWNER:
Mrs. Roy E. Satters
Phone: DEwey 9–7231
REWARD

But no one would answer that phone now. There would be no reward.

Several times the coyotes came back, but they

knew better than to try to take their home away
from this huge creature. At last the old male led
them to shelter in a strawstack a few miles to the
east.

The dog slept.

All night the blizzard howled, and when he
awakened in the morning it was still raging. The
onslaught of snow blotted out roads, covered
fences, filled ditches, and piled in mountainous
drifts that snapped telephone poles and trees.
Farmers were cut off from towns, and towns from
each other. Highway traffic ceased, and the trains
stopped running as the big rotary snowplows
stalled.

A hundred yards or so north of every exposed
section of east-and-west railroad or highway, snow
fences had been erected. These were slats woven
into strong wire, rolled up and stored away every
spring, set out again in the fall. They broke the
force of ordinary storms, piling up drifts which
themselves became bigger barricades to protect rail
lines and highways.

But no such fences could halt this storm. The
drifts quickly covered them, and then covered the
rails and highways.

Where man's wisdom had failed, the wild wisdom of the badger and coyote had been successful.
The badger who had originally made the hole in
which the dog had found shelter had dug it with
the entrance on the exposed south slope of the
gully wall. This was not so foolish as it looked,

16

because in a few hours the storm quickly covered this opening with a heavy snowdrift. This drift acted as a tight door that held out the icy cold, and held in the animal heat. The badger, perhaps with the aid of gophers, had also dug a ventilating tunnel up to the surface of the ground. Snow covered this too, but a certain amount of fresh air seeped through.

It was a comfortable den, not so warm as a bed by a steam radiator in a New York apartment; but here the big mutt was in no danger of freezing to death.

He looked out once that morning, breaking the drift with his big head, pulling it quickly back when he heard and felt the undiminished fury of the storm. Nature soon closed his door for him. He lay there most of the day, grieving for the people who had "lost" him.

Toward evening, the storm slackened. It was only a lull, and the weather-wise knew that the dampness in the air meant that worse was to come. But for a few hours it would be relatively calm.

The big dog could tell when the wind fell. For twenty hours he had lain in his stolen den, instinct warning him it was better to be hungry here than frozen elsewhere. Still, his appetite had grown ravenously. He still had reserves of fat on his ribs, but never in his life had he gone so long without food.

This time the heavy drift resisted his head. He had to dig his way through it. Once out, he stood in the bottom of the gully surrounded by drifts, looking up past the steeply cut banks to the black evening sky. He was not afraid, as a human being might have been afraid, because traffic and the kicks of strange people were all he had learned to fear. He did not hesitate. Boldly he sought the coyotes' zigzag path up the bank.

The path was not quite wide enough for him, but his big feet found a grip even where there was none. In a few moments he was back on the surface of the ground.

He did not know it, but he was already a wild dog.

He had in him generation after generation of hunting instinct, and only two years of discipline to make him a tame city dog.

Twenty lonely, grieving hours in a coyotes' den had stripped away those two years of tameness like so much excess fat. From centuries back in his ancestry came the knowledge of how to find the food his body needed.

He had never seen rabbits or gophers or prairie dogs. Anyway, the rabbits had not yet ventured out since the storm, and the gophers and prairie dogs were all deep in the ground in tunnels below the frost line, there to loaf in comfort, or to hibernate until spring.

But he remembered the sheep he had seen, and from somewhere deep in his fat, tame, lazy body came the knowledge that sheep were meat.

He started running, not hard but strongly, a patient pace he could keep up for a long time.

Something—another deeply buried instinct, used now for the first time—told him that he had not long to hunt before the snow fell again.

In a few minutes he reached the highway. He ran on, circling drifts. In a little while he came to the scent of sheep.

It was not the flock he had seen crossing the road, for these were still several miles to the east. This was a much smaller flock, not more than three or four hundred. They were sheltered in a small, crowded shed close to the highway. Nearby was a small stone house. A yellow light gleamed in its window, although night was still an hour or two away. This lamp had burned all day—as had lamps in houses for hundreds of miles around, all through this dark, long-to-be-remembered day of storm.

Somehow the dog knew better than to make a noise and arouse the human being whose shadow he saw crossing that yellow window. His keen nose led him straight to the sheepshed. His powerful legs lifted him lightly over the high fence, and he dropped inside the corral.

The dog knew it was wrong to dig in flower beds or to chase cars, but no one had ever told him that it was a serious crime for a hungry dog to kill a sheep. He knew only his great hunger. He feared the man in the little stone house as any trespassing city dog fears a stranger, but his fear was no worse than that.

The low, moaning wind tore noisily at the eaves

of the shed, muffling the jingle of the tags on his collar. The sheep bleated in terror as he glided in among them. They rushed for the corners in panic and piled on top of each other, the strong climbing over the weak. A few ran out into the storm and fell blindly into the drifts, where they stood, bleating senselessly.

The dog had never killed in his whole life.

Yet his ancestors had been killers for centuries, house dogs only for a few generations. He killed expertly, mercifully, like the good hunter nature had made him. The sheep he killed for food would have been killed, in just a few more months, by the man in the small stone house—and also for food.

Inside the house Bucky Turnbull, the vinegary old bachelor who owned this flock, was cleaning his rifle. He hated dogs, and was the only sheepman around here who would not have a sheep dog on the place. He thought he heard sheep bleating. He went to the window, opened it, and threw his flashlight's beam out over the corral.

A fat ewe was facing him, almost covered by the snowdrift into which she had fallen, scarcely a dozen feet away.

The man knew no sheep would leave shelter unless driven from it. He slammed the window down. Quickly he put the gun together. He slipped a load into the breech and ran out, in his haste forgetting to put on his shoes.

The dog heard the window slam. He did not

know that he was now a criminal—a sheep-killing dog, which to a sheepman is the worst criminal enemy of all. He did not know that he had made himself an outlaw, merely by taking the food that the man and woman had failed to supply.

But that slamming window, that startled yell—these were man sounds, things he knew well from his sometimes bitter experience with New York's teeming millions of people. He was full anyway. Up came his head, thinned out because of his fast. The chain choke collar, with the two brass tags, had slid down over his ears and had fallen in the snow beside the dead sheep.

He leaped the fence and streaked for the highway, running all the more strongly because he now had warm, life-giving meat in him. He heard Bucky Turnbull's shout of rage as he discovered the dead sheep, and he stored this up in his dog mind. Just as he must never let himself be caught digging in flower beds, so must he never let anyone catch him killing a sheep. To this extent, but no more, he knew he had been a "bad dog."

Just as the storm struck again, he came to his den in the gully. Food and exercise had been good for him. What he needed again was shelter. Already he had become storm-wise, as sleeping instincts awakened. He slid down the steep bank, jumped and floundered through the drifts to the door of his den, and crawled inside.

He slept once more.

Several times, while the storm was working up

new strength, the five coyotes came back. They had not found very warm quarters in the old strawstack, but they knew better than to try to drive out this powerful, meat-filled, big-jawed dog. At last they trotted back to the strawstack, in their own weather wisdom knowing that any shelter was better than none at all.

Back at the ranch, the old bachelor went in and put on his shoes. His flashlight batteries were weak, so he lighted a bright lantern and went out again, to drive his sheep back into the shed. Some of them were so drift-covered that he had to carry them . . . and then in panic they ran, and had to be carried in again.

At last they became quiet. Their simple minds had already forgotten the terror of a few moments ago. The old bachelor leaned down to shoulder the dead sheep, to carry it to his unheated porch. Much of this good mutton could be saved for his own use.

Suddenly his lantern caught a bright, brassy twinkle in the snow. It was the dog's collar. He took it inside, after disposing of the dead sheep.

"New York," he muttered as he studied it. "Wonder where Dwight Jerome got hold of this? I told Clay Jerome he'd be sorry if he let his kid bring that big wolfhound here. Now let him pay for it."

He went to the telephone and turned the crank as only an angry man could turn it.

"Hello, operator? Operator, give me three-three-two, Clayton Jerome's place. Operator, operator."

But the line was dead. A dozen poles were down, the wires snapped in a dozen places by the sheer weight of the storm. He hung up, went to the door, and looked out, a little fearfully.

"I'll be snowed in good by morning," he said to himself. "Well, there's nothing I can do about it until then, anyway."

The howling blizzard flung his words back at him. It chilled his little house and made his fire roar in the flue. He closed the door quickly.

CHAPTER THREE

THE MAN AND WOMAN who had abandoned the big dog soon forgot the boy with the flock of sheep, but he did not forget them. New York cars were rare here. Rarer still were dogs as big as the one he had seen in the back seat of the New York car.

Dwight Jerome had never lived anywhere except on the Badlands sheep ranch where his father, Clayton Jerome, had been born. North Dakota's raw winters and eternal winds, and the wild loneliness of the Badlands, had shaped and seasoned him. At fifteen, he was a short, wiry youth with dark hair, dark skin, and still darker freckles. He was strong for his age, and far more self-reliant than most city boys years older.

Dwight had many friends, not just among youngsters his own age, but among adults too. Yet the very traits that made people respect him also set him apart. His mother had noticed this early.

"Sometimes I think Dwight is half wild," she said impatiently, when he came home in the dark, after riding or tramping the Badlands all day. "When he gets out there alone he forgets the time, he forgets to be hungry, he forgets he's even got a home."

Dwight's father thought he understood his son better. He was a short, quiet, hard-working man who had also hunted the Badlands as a boy.

"Dwight would have made a good Indian fighter . . . or a good Indian," he said. "He's more at home with nature than any person I have ever known. Sometimes I think animals must talk to him."

Well, they didn't. Dwight knew that much.

But somehow he understood them, and they understood him. It was not a thing he could explain, but there was a link of sympathy between him and all wild, living things. It came from long observation of nature, from living with animals since babyhood in a wild, sparsely settled country.

All his life, his closest companions had been the tame ranch animals—sheep, dogs, and horses. All his life he had watched the little animals that were always being hunted—the chipmunks, rabbits, gophers, and prairie dogs. And he had watched the bigger animals that hunted them—the coyotes and snakes and skunks and badgers. He had grown up knowing them as most boys know the people next door.

To the man and woman who had dumped the big mutt out of their car, this country looked wild and empty. To Dwight it was full of living companions. To the man and woman, the fact that these wild things ate each other would have seemed cruel and savage. To Dwight it was perfectly natural, and not cruel at all.

Riding with his closest friend, Joe Turnbull, Dwight might suddenly rein in and say, "A coyote jumped a jack rabbit there—right next to that tuft of bluestem grass."

Joe, seeing nothing, would say, "How do you know?"

And Dwight would find it hard to answer. The things he saw—a blade of grass bent the wrong way, dirt where the coyote had lain and crept and inched forward, the small furrow dug by the terrified jack's hind foot as he jumped—no other eyes ever seemed to see them, somehow.

"I don't know," he would say, "but it got away, and old Mr. Coyote had to hunt his dinner somewhere else."

He knew these things because he had shared the perils of the rabbit, the hunger of the coyote.

He had lain for hours, without moving a muscle or making a sound, watching furtive little prairie dogs come out of their burrows and frisk about. He had watched the coyotes slip through the grass with tireless patience, moving so slowly that they seemed not to move at all. They paid no attention to him, either, regarding him as something as wild as themselves.

He had seen the coyotes pounce. He had seen the quick scurrying of the prairie dogs; he had seen the flash of teeth that ended in death for one of nature's little wild things. In nature, death is

merciful. Dwight had always known this. The cruel
way to die was man's way—the slow agony of
poison, or the festering of a gunshot wound that
did not quite hit and did not quite miss. That was
why he practiced so long, so often, with his rifle.
When he killed, he wanted to be at least as merciful as the coyote.

The coyotes he liked and admired, even though
he knew they were the sheepman's enemies, and
now and then must be killed.

Once he had inched his way up to the very
doorway of a burrow in the flat, open prairie where
his father cut hay. The spring winds were blowing,
the sun was warm, green grass was beginning to
hide the red earth of the Badlands, and there was a
fresh odor to the damp sod. To Dwight, it was
always good to be alive, but today it was better
than ever.

His face was perhaps a foot from the burrow,
when suddenly two bright eyes gleamed boldly out
of the black depths. He did not move. Not even the
wind rustling through his short hair startled the
owner of those two bright, beady eyes.

It was a mother coyote. They lay and watched
each other a moment. The eyes came closer, until
he could make out the sharp, foxlike face and
twitching nose. Still he did not move. She inched
still farther up, until one short step would have
brought her fangs within reach of his unprotected
face.

Down there in the depths of the ground she had

27

a litter of newborn pups. It was her first litter, or she would not have hidden them in a hole where the rain could run in freely. She had not been out of her den since their birth, and now she needed food and exercise.

She lay there, watching him. Then, from a little way behind him, Dwight heard the sharp, warning bark of her mate. He was telling her not to come out, but at the same time he seemed to be saying that everything would be all right if she simply did nothing.

Why didn't she attack him? Anyway, she did not, but went back down into her hole. Coyotes will fight, when their whelps are in danger. One slash of her teeth could have marked Dwight for life.

Still, he did not fear her, and she did not fear him—at least not much. Perhaps there is a smell to hatred, a smell that was missing about Dwight. Perhaps she sensed that he was just making a friendly, curious call.

The old he-coyote showed himself several times as Dwight went away. Dwight just laughed.

"Go on, I'm not going to chase you," he said. "You just want to draw me away from your pups, don't you? Quit worrying. Let our sheep alone and I'll let you alone."

He was a boy at peace, hating no one and nothing, looking down on nothing that lived as being below him. This was what his mother meant when she said he was half wild. This was what his father meant when he said he thought the animals talked to him.

They didn't really. Yet Dwight understood animals better than anyone in the country—better, even, than "Deputy Bill." Bill's real name was William Ehmken. He too had grown up on a sheep ranch. He had served four years overseas, with the Army in World War II. He had been wounded on Okinawa, but he brought back the gun that wounded him as a present for Dwight.

Once Bill too had roved the Badlands alone, lying in the grass and watching the endless adventure of nature, forgetting to come home for his meals. Now he was a strapping six-footer, a deputy sheriff who wore a badge, a six-shooter, and the Distinguished Service Cross.

"Don't you worry about Dwight," Deputy Bill told Mr. and Mrs. Jerome. "He'll turn out all right. A boy who knows the laws of nature isn't going to break the laws of man."

The first day of the big storm—the day Dwight had met the car and seen the big dog—he had been uneasy and restless in school. He found it hard to keep his mind on his work, and his eyes kept wanting to stray out of the window. A windbreak of ash trees grew north of the schoolhouse. He watched them bend and sway under the rising pressure of the wind.

This was a one-room country school, with only eight grades. Dwight and Joe Turnbull had graduated here the year before, but the nearest high school was forty miles away. Miss Stevenson, the teacher, had agreed to teach the boys their first year of high school. Next year they would have to board in town.

At the noon recess, Dwight could not stay inside, where the others were playing games. In range country, nothing is so important as the weather. His father's sheep were in a barley stubble field, across the highway and three miles south of the house. It was a flat, heart-shaped field between Badlands ridges and gullies. There was no shed, no protection if a storm hit.

And a storm was going to hit, Dwight knew suddenly. Perhaps his sympathy for all things in nature made him more keen to sense its approach. Or perhaps he only kept his eyes and ears open, and knew better how to understand what he saw and heard. Shortly after the noon recess, he went to the teacher and asked to be excused.

"But why, Dwight?" she asked.

Laura Stevenson was young and pretty and well liked, but she was new to the range country, and it was hard to make her understand. She came from Minneapolis. They had bad storms there too, but there was always some kind of protection from them. Here, there often was not.

"Because there's a blizzard making," said Dwight.

"But what makes you think so?" she asked, smiling.

30

For the life of him, he could not explain. "I just know. I—I *feel* it. Our sheep are in the barley stubble and ought to be brought in. Dad's gone to town."

"But, Dwight, I'm sure your sheep are all right."

"No, ma'am, they aren't. And I think Buddy Jacobs ought to go home and get their sheep in, and Joe Turnbull. It's been warm for a long time. We've all kept our sheep scattered, to save hay where we could. It—it's risky, Miss Stevenson. Please, I think we'd better go."

She was about to shake her head again, but she saw Joe Turnbull and Buddy Jacobs stand up. They were sheepmen's sons. They knew this odd, silent, likable boy better than she did.

"First, Dwight, let's see what the radio says."

She snapped the switch, and the announcer's voice filled the schoolroom.

This was the exact moment when, a few miles away, a man and a woman were listening to this same warning in a small, speeding car, in the back seat of which slept a big, fat, lazy dog.

Unlike the man and the woman, Miss Stevenson heard the warning through. She suddenly remembered stories she had heard of small children being lost in blizzards, on their way home from school.

"Would people think us foolish, Dwight, if we all went home?" she asked.

"No one will think you're foolish in Dakota,

ma'am, any time you try to beat a blizzard," said Dwight.

Now the school children were all home safely.

Now the sheep were all under shelter—the Jacobs sheep, and the Turnbull sheep too. People knew that "Dwight Jerome has kind of an Indian weather sense. When he says a storm is coming, watch out!"

Now Mrs. Jerome could say, this time proudly, "Yes, that boy of mine is half wild."

As Dwight followed the Jerome sheep home, he thought about the big mutt he had just seen in the New York car. He kept shouting, "Hi-you, hi-you, hi-you," letting his voice drop with each "you." The sheep heard this singsong chant, and knew they were safe. Feistie and Wrangle, the two sheep dogs, nipped and barked and hurried them, but the dogs were as familiar as Dwight's "Hi-you," and the sheep did not fear them.

Colleen, the big Irish wolfhound, could be heard baying hoarsely long before the sheep came into the yard.

Dwight had saved his money for a long time to send off for this expensive purebred. She was now almost three years old, and she had been a big disappointment. She had killed a few coyotes, but she was not a good hunter. Her heart was not in it. Too many of her ancestors had been chosen for the show ring, rather than for the chase.

Still, she was the biggest, handsomest dog in this

32

part of the country, and Dwight was fond of her.

"But she's not as big as that big mutt," he told himself as he plowed along behind the sheep, leaning into the storm. "Wonder what kind he was? . . . Hi-you, hi-you!"

A light was bobbing through the darkness. Dwight heard his father call: "In here, by the house gate. There isn't time to go around. Let's hurry, boy."

It would have taken only a few minutes longer to go down to the lower gate, but minutes counted. Feistie and Wrangle turned the sheep through the gate, and they raced down to the shelter of the shed. Mr. Jerome had already opened the corral for them. He leaned down to shout to his son:

"I got back late, but I knew I could count on you to bring in the sheep. This looks like a bad one."

"I saw a dog bigger than Colleen, Dad," Dwight shouted back.

"Save it until later."

There was other work to do, hard work, after the corral was closed and the sheep were safe. There were cows to be milked, eggs to be gathered, horses fed, coal brought to the house. A thick wire ran from the back door to the fence, to guide them to and from the house in just such storms. More than a few people had lost their lives in blizzards within a few yards of their own doors, with no wire to guide them.

Feistie and Wrangle bedded down with the

33

sheep. No one would bring them food until the storm eased, but empty stomachs were not new to them. No matter what happened they would stay with the sheep.

Feistie's mother was buried, with six other faithful sheep dogs, in a little plot in the grove north of the sheepshed. She had frozen to death, trying to bring five lost sheep home through a storm like this one. Wrangle was blind in one eye from a fight with coyotes who had raided the lamb pens two summers ago.

Feistie and Wrangle were old dogs, not house pets, but valuable workers, respected as well as loved. They were no breed or all breeds, like most sheep dogs in this country. Perhaps all shared a strain of collie; certainly they all shared the old-fashioned collie's herding instinct and lionhearted devotion to duty.

"What's this about a big dog, Dwight?" the father asked, as they removed their coats in the house, after the work was done.

Dwight told him about the car with the New York license plates, and the brindle mutt with the hound ears and the huge jaws and feet.

Dwight's three younger sisters listened eagerly. Irene was thirteen; Christine, eleven; and June, or "Trinket," four. Like all sheepmen's children, they were interested in anything about a dog. Their eyes grew round as Dwight described the one he had seen this afternoon.

"What a wolf dog he'd make!" Dwight said.

"Why, he was big enough for Trinket to saddle and ride!"

"You're not going to bring another dog here," said his mother, only partly overhearing.

Mr. Jerome smiled. "I should hope not. We've already got dogs enough to do us. Look at that big, useless creature there."

He pointed to Colleen, sleeping behind the stove. Trinket, who considered Colleen her special friend, sat down heavily on the big hound's ribs. Colleen stirred and groaned, but was careful not to upset the child.

"She's not useless," Christine said stoutly. "She takes good care of Trinket, anyway."

"And maybe someday she'll be a wolf dog," said Irene.

Their father had complained of Colleen before. The girls had ready answers for him each time.

"Everything that lives must earn its way," Mr. Jerome said. "The sheep dogs earn theirs, and Colleen should too. Listen to that wind! I pity any living thing that hasn't a warm bed tonight."

All night, and all the next morning, the snow swirled down on the howling wind. There was no school. The sky cleared suddenly about noon, and the sun shone brightly on a world that glistened white and dead and still.

Irene and Christine put on overalls, overshoes, and mittens, to help clear paths through the snow.

"Although," the father said soberly, "it'll probably be wasted work. Radio says this storm reaches a thousand miles north, and it'll take a week for it to pass over us."

There were paths to dig to the chicken house, grain bin, barn, sheepshed, and coal shed. In this part of North Dakota, thick seams of a coarse, soft coal, called lignite, broke through the earth in many places. The Jeromes had such a seam, a hundred feet from the house. It had been roofed over, and as they dug into the seam, steps were cut in the coal. Two generations had dug coal here, and the pit was now twenty feet deep, a dozen wide, and half again as long.

Down there it was dark and warm and cozy, The girls, filling boxes and buckets to last through the longest storm, took their time.

This was Colleen's favorite daytime den too. She bounded up ahead of the girls when they ran to tell their father that the boxes were full. A jack rabbit came hopping unwarily into the yard. Colleen chased him into a drift and caught him easily. Later, when this snow settled and crusted, the rabbits would skim lightly over the top, while dogs fell through. Now Colleen's long legs gave her the advantage.

"I wish she was good for something besides chasing jacks," said Mr. Jerome. "We'll have trouble at lambing time. The coyotes are lean enough already. They'll be starving. A good wolf dog would be worth her weight in gold."

He harnessed a team, and, with Dwight's help, dragged a wide path down to the sheepshed. They hauled more baled hay, more sacked barley, into the shelter of the shed. And just in time, for by late afternoon it had started to snow gently again.

Gently . . . but far to the north there was a low moaning sound. As they put their team away, they felt the first blast rock the barn. As they sat down to supper, the storm hit with all of its old-time fury.

Dwight slept alone in a little attic room, reached by a ladder that ran up one kitchen wall. He awakened early, cold despite the heavy blankets and comforters that covered him. The world was strangely silent. He had gone to sleep with the howl of the blizzard in his ears. Now, the moon was shining brightly through his north window.

Teeth chattering, Dwight sat up and looked out in amazement. One towering drift stretched from a corner of the house all the way to the sheepshed. It was so high that he could have opened his window and reached it with his arm.

He struck a match and glanced at his watch. It was ten minutes after five. He got out of bed, shivering, and shoved his clothing through the trap door. He did not wait to climb down the ladder, but swung through it and dropped to the icy floor.

By the time his father awakened, Dwight had the fires roaring with fresh lignite. The house was warm. Mr. Jerome went to the window and peered out, shaking his head.

"It's the worst I've ever seen," he said.

Colleen stood up behind the stove, growling softly. From outside came a man's voice.

"Clay! Clay Jerome! Anybody awake? Clay, come out here."

Mr. Jerome chuckled. "Bucky Turnbull, and mad as a hornet again. Must be pretty upset to be out this early."

Bucky was Joe's bachelor uncle, and the Jeromes' nearest neighbor. He hated dogs, and lived alone in a small stone house, with his sheep corral just outside his window.

Mr. Jerome slipped into a coat and went outside. Dwight followed, pushing Colleen back into the house, knowing Bucky's hatred of her.

The old man sat on a tired, sweaty, steaming horse in the front yard. The moonlight twinkled on the six gun in his hand. His face, swathed in his scarf, could not be seen, but his voice was harsh with anger.

"Better get that kid in the house, Clay," he said, "and then call that big dog of his out here. I'm going to shoot her."

"Oh, you are, are you?" Mr. Jerome said quietly. "Mind saying why?"

"Because she killed a sheep for me, that's why!" Bucky shouted angrily. "Came right up to the house night before last. I haven't been able to dig my way out until now. I want to be paid for that

38

sheep, Clay, and I want that dog killed. I've got her collar to prove it's her."

Mr. Jerome walked down and laid his hand on Bucky's horse. "I don't know what killed your sheep, but it wasn't Colleen. She was in the house all night, and she's still got her collar."

"Then what do you call this?"

Bucky dangled the chain choke collar, with its two tags, in Mr. Jerome's face. Mr. Jerome examined it.

"It's not hers, Bucky. Dwight saw a big mutt in a tourist's car last Monday evening, over on the state highway. It was a New York car and this is a New York license. Be reasonable, Bucky. Suppose I come over and see what this looks like?"

"All right," Bucky grumbled. "I left the house at midnight, but I've broken a path so it shouldn't take you so long."

"I'm going too," said Dwight.

It was ten o'clock before Dwight and his father returned. The three girls met them at the door. Mrs. Jerome had heard Bucky shouting, and had warned them to keep Colleen in the house until their father returned.

"You can let her out now," the father said. "It wasn't Colleen, and Bucky knows it now."

"What was it, a timber wolf?" Mrs. Jerome asked. "One of those big, gray Saskatchewan cruisers?"

"No. I'd know a wolf track, and we haven't had

any Canadian wolves down here for years. It was a dog."

"Oh, dear, a sheep-killing dog! But maybe the storm got him."

Mr. Jerome shook his head. He had seen other sheep-killing dogs. Perhaps they killed only for food, at first. But sooner or later a savage murder lust seemed to come over them, so that they killed only for the cruel sport of killing, sometimes destroying whole flocks in a single night.

"I'm afraid not," Mr. Jerome said thoughtfully. "He's too smart for that. We're likely to hear a lot more of this fellow before we hear the last of him."

CHAPTER FOUR

THE DOG HAD BEEN DUMPED OUT OF THE CAR, and had luckily found the coyotes' den, on a Monday night.

It was on the following night, Tuesday, that he killed Bucky Turnbull's sheep. Time on a calendar meant nothing to him. He measured his time by hunger and thirst, by weariness and rest. All Wednesday morning he lay in his den, his somewhat shaggy tail curled around his tender nose—exactly as the wolf creatures far, far back in his ancestry had protected their tender noses.

When, that Wednesday, the storm cleared briefly, he came out of his den once more, breaking through the barrier of snow with a great, leaping rush. But somehow he was now unsure of himself by daylight. He sensed that this was not the end of the storm, but only another lull. Fear of being seen, as well as fear of the storm, made him crawl back into his den, after gulping a little snow.

He slept soundly all night. The next morning his great hunger drove him out into daylight, and at the time Dwight and his father were riding with Bucky to see Bucky's dead sheep, the dog was

42

loping across the Badlands scarcely a quarter of a mile away. Their voices came to him on the clear, cold air, but he made sure to stay out of their sight.

He had already forgotten the two people who had abandoned him here. He had been too long on a chain, too long kept in small rooms, too long disciplined as a big dog must be disciplined in a crowded city. Having lost the collar he had worn all his life, he felt free. He liked being free, and he swerved away from Bucky Turnbull's place. He feared the three riders would put him back on a chain because he had been a "bad dog" there.

He loped on. In broad daylight he approached Vaughn Jacobs' place. The Jacobs sheepsheds were in a sheltered valley a quarter of a mile south of the house. Several years back, Mr. Jacobs had planted a windbreak of hardy Canadian pines around it. The dog circled the ranch carefully and came in through these trees.

Buddy Jacobs, one of the boys who had left school the day the storm broke, to bring in the sheep, was a year younger than Dwight Jerome. He had a sore throat that day and was being kept indoors. His father and Walt Trescoli, the hired man, were grinding fodder up by the barn. The chugging of the tractor engine came clearly to the bit mutt as he lurked in the pines, sampling the wintry air, sensing danger and trying to locate it with his keen nose.

After a moment he turned, circled the sheep-shed, and scrambled over the corral fence. The

Jacobses had only one sheep dog, a small, loyal nipper whose courageous heart was too big for his body. He leaped for the big mutt's throat, but the mutt ignored him. All his life, small dogs had insulted him, and he had learned to pay no attention to them. He did not even bother to attack the nipper, even when it slashed at him again and again, barking frantically.

He killed expertly and ate rapidly, like the wild hunter he had already become.

Up by the barn, the fodder mill shook and rattled, the tractor chugged away noisily. But Walt Trescoli, when he stepped away from the mill to cough up some dust, thought he heard something. He went a little farther from the tractor and lifted his ear flaps, listening, frowning, staring down at the sheepshed.

He could see nothing there, and the tractor drowned out every other noise. Still, it *did* sound as though the dog was yapping at something. He went back and tapped Mr. Jacobs' shoulder, shouting into his ear.

"Jake, sounds like something's scaring the sheep. I thought I heard the dog bark."

"I can't imagine what it could be, right out in broad daylight," Mr. Jacobs said.

Nevertheless, he throttled the engine down and walked a few yards away, to watch and listen.

His face turned white. He yelled: "Get the rifle, Walt. Must be a wolf."

He began to run down the slope toward the

44

sheepshed, shouting in fear as the blatting of the sheep, the barking of the dog, now came clearly. Walt raced into the house and snatched the .30-30 rifle from its pegs. When he came out with it, Mr. Jacobs was pointing down toward the pines.

"Great Scott, will you look at that!" Walt cried.

The big mutt came out of the trees and crossed the little snow-covered valley boldly, knowing they would never lay hands on him now.

Walt was a crack shot. The dog did not know what a rifle was, but he heard Walt shout. He ran a little faster, but he still did not stretch himself.

Walt threw himself down on the ground on his stomach. He sighted along the barrel. The big mutt heard the sharp twang-ng-ng-ng of the bullet, and something struck his hind leg with paralyzing force. He yelped and tumbled headlong into the snow.

Then came the billowing, booming echo of the gun.

His fall saved the dog from Walt's quick, deadly second shot. He howled and twisted in the snow, snapping at his wound. The bullet had cut a clean furrow across his leg without doing any real damage. Pain there was, more than he had ever felt in his life, but no real danger.

The danger, he sensed, came in that second sharp twang-ng-ng-ng that came as he writhed and howled in the snow. He hurled himself to his feet and began to run.

He was gone before Walt could draw another

bead. He was running strongly, on all four legs, when he reached the empty, drifted highway.

Here he stopped to lick his wound, to puzzle over this new, strange, terrible danger. Here he was when he saw Vaughn Jacobs ride out to spread the alarm that a huge, sheep-killing, outlaw dog was loose on the country.

The dog did not know that he was now doubly an outlaw, and that Vaughn Jacobs could reach a working telephone, as Bucky could not, that other night. He only knew that he had to live.

He did not even argue that he had a right to live—that he had been dumped out in the worst blizzard in history by people who said, "It's the kindest thing, after all."

All the dog knew was that he had been punished until the blood flowed. Hereafter, wherever there was the gun scent, or the crack of guns, or the spiteful twang of bullets, he would feel that death was not far away.

Wounded, frightened, and weary, but at least no longer hungry, he went back to his den. The five coyotes had unwisely moved into it. He attacked them savagely, scattering them like flies. They streamed up the zigzag path, faster than he could follow them in his rage.

The dog crawled into the den and lay there licking his wounded leg. At last he slept, but in his sleep he twitched nervously, dreaming of guns.

By evening, word of his two killings had spread over the entire, snow-bound county.

Sheriff Cecil Lang, old, gray-haired, plump and easygoing, came out to investigate Vaughn Jacobs' report about a huge dog. "As big as a yearling colt," Mr. Jacobs had said.

While the sheriff was there, Bucky Turnbull rode in with the lost dog collar. Hating dogs bitterly, he demanded that Sheriff Lang drop everything else and hunt down the sheep killer. The sheriff put the chain choke collar in his pocket.

"All right, Bucky," he said. "I'll call this New York number, and see if the people have any relatives around here. Maybe we can run him down that way."

Bucky shook his fist. "You'd better do a lot more than that. Where's Bill Ehmken, the mighty hunter? Why don't you get him out on the job? What are the taxpayers paying him a salary for?"

"I said I'd get busy, Bucky."

Back at his office, the sheriff put in a call for the New York number.

"I'm sorry, that telephone has been disconnected," said a girl nearly two thousand miles away.

The sheriff hung up, sighing. "I was afraid that was how it would be." He had been a sheepman himself. He remembered other sheep-killing dogs, and the waves of trouble that followed their night raids. An outlaw dog "as big as a yearling colt" would bring terror to people already bewildered by the great storm.

47

No dog was that big, the sheriff knew. Yet people would believe anything at times.

He was almost grateful when it began to snow again that evening. Even sheep-killing dogs would be marooned—while new drifts piled on drifts already the largest in the memory of man—while trains gave up trying to run as their crews sought shelter anywhere—while more thousands of miles of Western highways were closed, beyond the puny power of the snowplows to open them.

For three more days the blizzard howled, and for these three days, nothing more was heard from the big outlaw mutt.

All this time, the dog remained in his den. On the fourth day, when the weather finally cleared, he came out. By the time he had scrambled painfully up the snow-covered path to the surface of the ground, he was used to the slight inconvenience of his wound. He only walked a little stiffly. The pain he ignored.

He was gaunt and thin. The last of the fat he had stored during his easy city life had been used up. Instinct had made him lie quietly until his leg healed and the storm had ceased. That same instinct now told him that his very life depended upon his quickly finding food, before it could storm again. He turned about slowly, anxiously sniffing the still, icy air.

Not a single thing moved in this world of sparkling arctic white. The sun shone brightly, but without warmth, on a mighty mantle of snow that stretched unbroken from the Texas Panhandle to the North Pole. Haystacks were smooth, white cones, like the meringue-covered tarts the woman used to feed the dog as they walked home from shopping trips, back in New York. Fences had long since vanished. The trees were nearly buried by drifts, their brittle, wintry branches crushed and twisted by the immense burden of snow. A few telephone poles leaned at crazy angles out of the oddly swirled drifts.

The world lay cold and lifeless, with a new shape, one tweaked and twisted by the nimble fingers of the north wind. A lover of landscapes could have been thrilled by this view, but the dog knew nothing of beauty. All he knew, at the moment, was a vast, gnawing hunger.

The highway, too, had disappeared, but the dog headed in that direction. He skirted drifts when he could. When he could not, the gnaw of hunger drove him through or over them on three legs. The road meant ranches, ranches meant sheep, sheep meant food. Nothing but food mattered.

He found the road at last—or at least a short, bare, wind-swept section of it. Here high drifts again barred his way. He trotted back and forth, for his sore leg's sake, seeking the easiest way through.

Suddenly a scent made the dog cringe and turn, growling, not in fear or anger but in the sheer excitement of hunger. He leaped awkwardly through the drifts, forgetting all about his wound. He came to another bare patch of pavement and here he stopped and put his nose out, trying to solve the riddle before him.

Three steers had stopped to rest here, while the great storm was at its worst. They had turned their tails to the wind and huddled with their heads down. Now they were almost covered with snow. They were facing the dog as he came floundering through the drifts.

He approached them warily. He had never attacked cattle before, and these three motionless white heads, with their short, wicked horns, carried their own warning.

An inch at a time he crept toward them. Still the steers did not move . . . nor would they ever move again.

They were dead. They had wandered before the storm until their strength gave out. Here they had frozen to death on their feet, leaning against each other with their heavy, horned heads turned toward the south. The storm had played its cruel joke to the limit. It had packed snow under and around and on them until their frozen bodies could not fall down. They stood stiffly dead, in deep and sightless silence menacing a dead, white world.

But they were meat—food that even a wounded dog could claim, food to be had without the awful risk and terror of gunfire.

The starving coyotes were not far behind the big mutt. They came slinking in from all sides, whimpering and chattering. Their ribs stood out starkly. The storm had not used them kindly, either.

At first the dog drove them away, but they were too many for him, and too hungry. Hunger made a truce. At last they feasted together, the tall dog ignoring his half-starved, bickering little wild relatives.

Suddenly the bickering stopped. The coyotes cringed to the snow. Every pointed face turned to the north, and every little pointed ear shot forward. A wise old he-coyote growled a warning.

The dog too shot his ears forward as a long, low moan came quivering eerily over the snow. He had never before heard a wolf, but he did not need to be told that here was a bitter, fierce, vengeful enemy with whom there could never be a truce. Centuries ago, the dog's wild ancestors had given up their wildness, to come to the firesides of man. The wolves had stayed away, their fierceness growing fiercer as the dogs then helped the men hunt them down. The dog's ancestors had heard that same moaning hunger cry centuries ago. They too had bristled and snarled, just as the big mutt did now.

Two gaunt, gray shapes came gliding over the snow. They reached the pavement, scarcely a hundred yards away. They were real Saskatchewan cruisers, prairie wolves rather than timber wolves, and experienced hunters of livestock. Long before this great storm hit the Badlands, it had laid its icy, iron hand on the prairie provinces of Canada.

51

It had driven this thin, reckless pair of killers before it for a thousand miles. With every mile they had grown thinner, and more reckless.

The coyotes scattered soundlessly, leaving the big dog to face the wolves alone.

The dog had been a wild dog for several days, killing his own meat and hiding in a wild den. Yet, as these still wilder creatures appeared, it was the outraged instincts of a tame dog that came to the surface. This was his meat! He took a step toward the wolves, growling noisily.

The wolves crouched in the snow and waited for him. When he came close enough, one of them would slash at him and leap away; and as he turned to defend himself, the other would cut him down from behind. He had never fought wolves, but somehow he knew this was how it would be.

But before it could happen, a sound came rapping sharply through the still, wintry air. Clayton Jerome was fixing a window in his barn, miles to the north, his hammer booming on the closed barn like a drumstick on a drum. It was a man sound, a tame sound, and it made the tame dog bolder, the wild wolves wilder.

The dog charged, baying as only a big hound can bay. The wolves fled, but they ran as much from the sound of the man's hammer as they did from the dog. They had no way of knowing that the dog too was an outlaw, as badly hated as they were. They knew only that they were in man's country, and here was some man's dog raising an alarm.

Miles to the north, Clayton Jerome heard that bell-like baying. He stopped hammering to listen.

"There's no prettier music than the sound of a good hound on a hot trail, is there?" he said.

Dwight frowned, lifting his ear flaps to hear better. "I don't recognize that one, though, and I thought I knew every dog in the country. I wonder if it's that big New York mutt, the sheep killer?"

"I doubt it," said the father. "A sheep killer barks a kind of shrill, crazy, hysterical bark, when he makes any sound at all. This fellow's in a hurry. He's chasing something that gets around faster than a sheep."

He listened a moment and then began to hammer again.

The wolves, nearing the Badlands, had separated, knowing the dog could follow only one of them. He followed the she-wolf. The male saw this, and turned. He began angling in. For a moment, they almost cornered the big mutt between them.

That was when Mr. Jerome began hammering again.

The wolves ran. Greater than hunger was their deep-seated terror of man. Food could come later. What counted now was to get away from this big, noisy dog and that terrifying hammer sound.

The dog loped along behind them, driving them

into the Badlands, sounding his alarm long after there was no ear within hearing distance.

They were too fast for him, and too smart. When he came close, they separated, trying to lure him between them. Finally they gave up doing this, and just ran. While one led the dog on and on and on, the other rested. Then they crossed trails, and between them they wore him down. The dog had never hunted before. He learned quickly, but not quickly enough to keep from wasting his strength in useless miles of running.

Still, he at least had strength to waste, being newly fed, while the wolves had run a thousand miles with famine at their heels. They remembered their hunger as they outdistanced him. Little by little they circled eastward, and then back to the south, so that when night fell they would once more be within striking distance of livestock.

Still the dog clung to their trail. He was learning, little by little, how to cope with the problem they left when they crossed trails. Now he could tell their trails apart. Deep in his strong hunter's body was a hunter's intelligence and wisdom. Now, when they broke their trail, he circled widely until he picked up the scent he had been following on the other side of the break.

By dark, the wolves had stopped trying to play tricks on him. By dark the dog too had stopped wasting his breath. He no longer bayed as he ran.

The moon came up. The wolves doubled north— and then again turned south. They came close to the Jerome ranch, and a sudden shift of the night wind brought their wild scent clearly to the sheep dogs.

The big mutt heard the shrill barking of Feistie and Wrangle. He remembered the bullets, the pain, the frightening crack of the rifle. He dared follow the wolves no closer.

But he was, after all, a man's dog. All his life, men had solved his problems for him. Here was one too big for his simple brute mind. Wolves were prowling and he dared come no closer to do anything about it.

He sat down and pointed his nose at the moon and howled. In the only way he knew, he told the sleeping world of mankind to beware of the wolves.

CHAPTER FIVE

LONG AFTER THE REST OF THE FAMILY WERE asleep, Dwight lay awake in his attic room, looking out over the moonlit Badlands.

The fires were banked downstairs. The house was cold, but he was heavily covered to the chin. His breath froze quickly on blankets and window glass. Now and then he put out his hand to scrape the glass with his thumbnail, putting it back under the covers quickly as he felt the deadly bite of the cold.

Thirty degrees below zero was not uncommon here; his senses told him that it was much colder tonight.

He knew every foot of the Badlands that showed through his small, frosty window, yet now they looked as wild and strange as a map of the moon. Miss Stevenson had shown them a picture of part of the moon's surface taken through a giant telescope. The moon was cold and dead, she said. Nothing could live there. "Like the Badlands," she explained.

Dwight chuckled. He knew these Badlands were

not dead, but only sleeping. Below the snow the fiery-red earth was the same. Below the frost line, four or five feet down, the Badlands' teeming millions slept their warm winter sleep. They would come up cautiously with the spring, following the frost as the sun drew it from the ground. When they popped out at last, followed by their winter-born babies who were getting their first view of the world of sun and wind, there would be green, tender food of a new growing season waiting for them.

Nature took care of its own. Where it took one thing away, it gave something in return. Dwight knew this.

So the Badlands were not lonely, dead, and lifeless, to him. Those were his friends down there in the red earth, and they were just as safe and warm and comfortable in their snug beds as he was in his. They fared better in their Badlands, in fact, than his own kind had lately. The radio this evening had summed up the hundreds of thousands of sheep and cattle and horses already killed all over the West by this unbelievable storm.

Dwight did not know what awakened him. The first thing he knew he was sitting up in bed. He was shivering, but not from cold. His pulse was pounding strongly. His scalp tingled. The moon was still high and bright. His big nickel watch, dangling by its chain from his iron bedstead, told him it was one o'clock.

As he sat listening, shivering, tingling, a sound came to him—a wild, strange, wavering howl, out of the Badlands. *And not far away, either,* he thought, as he slid out of bed. He groped his way down the ladder in the dark and tapped at his parents' bedroom door. His father answered sleepily.

"What's the matter, Son?"

"Come out here a minute and listen, Dad. I want you to hear what I heard."

"What is it?"

"I don't know. I think Feistie and Wrangle woke me up, barking, but I'm not sure. Then I heard something else."

Mr. Jerome came out. They went to the back door, opened it, and stood listening together.

Soon the sound came again, clear and close.

"What is it, timber wolf?" Dwight whispered.

His father shook his head. "I don't think so. In fact, I'm sure it isn't. I haven't heard one for years and years, but I'd know it. That sounds more like that big outlaw dog, howling at the moon."

"He's not very far from here."

"I know, and I don't like it."

"Look at Colleen."

The wolfhound had come up behind them. She whimpered softly and waved her shaggy tail as the howl quivered through the night. Down at the sheepshed, Feistie barked uneasily. A restless sheep blatted.

"It's a dog, all right; Colleen can tell the difference," said Mr. Jerome. "There's plenty of moonlight left. Maybe I can get a shot at him, but I don't want him coming in behind my back while I'm out hunting him.

"Get dressed, and build up the fires and stay awake. Put Colleen outside, where she can raise a racket if she hears anything. I'll open the coalpit door, so she'll be warm. If you don't hear anything from me before I go, you'll know everything is all right with the sheep."

He dressed and went out, carrying his rifle. Dwight heard him saddling his bay horse, Sparrow, in the corral. He listened carefully, but after that he heard nothing.

Everything was all right down at the sheepshed, then.

Dwight built up the fires and sat down by the kitchen stove. Soon he was drowsing in his chair.

Hours later, his father returned. It was not quite daylight when Dwight heard him stirring up the fire in the water tank heater down by the corral. Dwight dressed and ran outside.

"Did you see him, Dad?"

"No," his father said somberly, "but I saw where he'd just been. Didn't Colleen make a fuss?"

"No. Look, she's been in the coalpit all the time— I can tell by her tracks. He didn't get into our sheep?"

"We've got eleven dead ones," the father said grimly. "They were all right when I left. He must have slipped in behind me while I was out hunting him. That's bold and smart. Dwight, that dog's got the Bad Spirit in him, as the Indians used to say. That's a sheep killer for you. They start with one or two, but soon it's a dozen, and then a hundred."

"I can't understand why Colleen didn't make a fuss," Dwight said. "She should have heard Feistie and Wrangle, anyway."

"Feistie and Wrangle are dead."

"Oh, no!"

"Yes. He killed them first. I don't know how he did it without making some kind of noise, but he did."

"O Dad!" Dwight was fifteen, yet still the tears came. He had grown up with the sheep dogs. "Let me try to get him. You said yourself that I'm a better hunter than you are."

He was surprised when his father said, in a tired voice: "All right, but not now. The moon's going down and it's a long time until sunrise. Get started early in the morning. Take Colleen with you. Watch sharp, boy. Try to get in a shot at him. Even if you don't hit him, let him know he's being hunted."

Long before daylight Dwight was dressed and out of the house. He carried his precious rifle under his arm. It was a fine prewar Arisaka 6.5, rechambered for standard American ammunition. The barrel had been shortened and American sports sights attached. It was a light, short gun, ideal for the saddle, accurate and with real killing power.

It was too much trouble to heat milk, so he had filled his thermos bottle with hot water from the teakettle that always stood on the stove. Into the hot water went a tea bag and some sugar. He ate a few slices of bread before he saddled Limpy.

Limpy was his own horse, a fine pinto formerly owned by a wealthy rancher near here. The man had turned down hundreds of dollars for him as a colt, but the horse suddenly went lame just as he was being broken to the saddle.

"What'll you take for him?" Dwight had asked then.

"Son, you don't want a lame horse."

"I want this one, sir."

"Then take him for nothing. He's coyote bait."

Dwight shook his head. "I don't think he's lame at all. He's faking it. He's lazy, and just smart enough to pretend a limp to get out of work."

The man laughed. "If he's that smart, and if you're smart enough to make a useful horse out of him, you're welcome. Take him for nothing."

And now Limpy limped when he thought he could get away with it . . . but he had four good legs when Dwight rode him.

Dwight put Colleen on a chain and led her and the pinto down to the sheepshed. The hound thought a romp was coming, and wanted to run. Dwight tied the horse to the corral fence, took the lantern from the peg where it always hung, lighted it, and led Colleen inside.

What he saw made him sick, but it also made

him pinch his lip and study the ground thoughtfully. There was something strange about Colleen's actions too. It seemed mighty funny that she'd wag her tail and whine when she heard the big mutt howl last night, and then snarl at his scent this morning.

And it looked mighty funny, the way Feistie and Wrangle had been killed.

"They never knew what hit them," Dwight said. "How could one be killed without the other hearing? Maybe there are *two* sheep-killing dogs. But two smart enough—and big enough—to kill Feistie and Wrangle that quickly?"

A long time he knelt there, moving the lantern over the dust that lay thick inside the sheltered shed. The sheep, their panic long forgotten, remained calm. They were used to his quiet presence. Colleen whined and tugged at the chain. On his knees Dwight tried to follow the tracks, holding Colleen with one hand, the lantern with the other.

"They sure don't look like the tracks at Bucky Turnbull's place," he muttered. "They're longer, and not nearly so wide. And it seems like those tracks at Bucky's showed the nails had been clipped."

Wolf?

But his father knew a wolf's howl, and he had been quite positive that it was a dog baying in the Badlands last night.

Dwight climbed into the saddle and looped Colleen's chain securely around the saddle horn. He let the big hound lead the way. He rode leaning out of the saddle, studying the tracks by the light of the dangling lantern. Limpy paced along sedately. Suddenly, there were *two* sets of tracks in the snow. Dwight stopped in amazement.

Had the outlaw mutt found a wolf mate, perhaps? It didn't make sense. Yet there had to be some explanation. Feistie and Wrangle had been slashed to pieces. Dwight shook his head.

"That dog might slash once in a while, but he's mostly a gripper," he said to himself. "He'd grab a little dog and shake it to death, while it howled its head off. Colleen would have heard that. So would I."

Suddenly Colleen veered off through the snow, and Dwight's scalp tingled as he looked down and saw only one set of tracks again. The hound pulled hard, whining in her throat. Dwight stopped Limpy a moment, to try to figure this out. Two killers . . . yet only one had left the shed.

Why?

In a moment he understood. The second animal had been following the first one, stepping carefully in its tracks!

Now he knew it was wolves. Not coyotes, but those big Saskatchewan cruisers they used to have here in the old days, when his father was a boy— shrewd, smart, savage killers who could hunt alone, or in pairs, or in whole family packs. No more vicious killer lived in nature.

Then where was the big mutt?

Suddenly he knew what had happened, as clearly as if he had seen it. A boy who was half wild could sense what had happened to a half-wild dog.

The big mutt had been following the wild wolf scent. He had come as close to a ranch as he dared, and there he had howled, as any dog would howl! And while Dwight's father was out hunting the dog, the two wolves had slipped in boldly and made their kills.

"I know it!" Dwight said excitedly. "I know that's what happened . . . and pretty soon I'll find the dog's tracks too. Then I can be sure. . . ."

The eastern sky was gray. Dwight dropped the lantern into the snow, where he could find it on his return. He untied Colleen and spurred Limpy after her as the big, rangy hound flashed away.

Colleen had never shown much interest in tracking before, but now she ran swiftly, with her nose to the ground. The one set of tracks again became two. The boy drove the pinto hard, following a trail that went straight as an arrow, ever deeper and deeper into the heart of the Badlands.

Presently he came to the big mutt's tracks, just as he had known he would. The hound had waited off there to the west, and then began circling for scent. He had picked up the trail here, and was up there ahead somewhere, between Dwight and the wolves.

Dwight forgot to be hungry.

Broad daylight found him in a strange and lonely place. Colleen had settled down to a long, effortless lope. The boy looked around. To the west some thirty miles lay Montana. To the north, not much farther away, was Canada, another country, with a king instead of a president, a Parliament instead of a Congress, and a flag of its own. Across that other country's line these alien killers had come boldly, forced ever farther southward by starvation, as the storm laid its terrible hand on the deep north.

Dwight's father had long ago taught him how nature struck its own balances, sometimes with the help of man, sometimes in spite of him. Nature was life, was a law above law. In all things, it demanded balance.

"Coyotes would rather eat varmints, mice and prairie dogs and gophers and chipmunks and rabbits, even grasshoppers," Mr. Jerome had said.

"But we brought in sheep, and the sheep ate the grass and brush that used to feed the varmints, so there weren't as many of them as before. A few coyotes went hungry. Then we put out poison to kill still more varmints, to save the range for our sheep, and pretty soon there wasn't anything for the coyote to eat.

"When he can get anything else, the coyote won't bother our stock, but when he's hungry he's going to eat.

"Likewise with those big wolves up north. Game is what they want—moose and deer, rabbits and grouse, fish and mice—and berries. Anything they can get. But when they have a bad winter the game has to move south, or starve, the leaf eaters hunting for leaves, the meat eaters hunting the leaf eaters. And they're not going to starve when they get here, either.

"Man can disturb the balance, but sooner or later nature throws in more weights on her side, with snow or drought or floods or fire. Sometimes these disasters drive men out. The wild things come back. Sometimes disasters merely cut us down to size, and only a few wild things come back. But there is always balance."

This storm, swooping down from Athabasca, was a heavy weight thrown into the balance by nature. It had restored old natural forces, overruling man's laws as well as his desires. Those wolf tracks in the snow—they were part of nature's answer to man, who had killed off the small game here.

"See?" nature seemed to be saying to Dwight. "You're not so smart, are you?"

And Dwight, as Limpy cantered on and on and on, shook his head soberly, thinking: *No, we're not. Not half as smart as that dog. We need him on our side. Jeepers, will you look at the size of those tracks . . . !*

CHAPTER SIX

NOW AND THEN DWIGHT MADE COLLEEN REST while he rested Limpy. The pinto smelled the wolf smell too and wanted to go home. But Colleen tried to press on eagerly. All her hunting traits had come out suddenly. She resented having to stop, while those two trails lured her on.

As he rested, Dwight filled the cup from his thermos bottle with snow, poured in a little hot tea, and added more snow. It was all he needed to warm and refresh him. When he became hungry, he simply cinched up his belt and rode on, putting food out of his mind.

After each rest, before mounting his horse, he tried the action of the Arisaka. His hand was never far from the smooth walnut gunstock that protruded from the saddle boot.

Soon the tracks veered sharply, as though the wolves were circling back to where they would again be close to food. By now Dwight had no hope of catching them. Wolves holed up by daylight, but they could travel a lot of miles before they had to do so. They would still be far ahead of him when the approach of night would make it necessary for him to go home.

The dog, though, was another story. As nearly as he could judge, the big mutt was never far behind the two marauders. He was getting tired, and taking shorter steps. So was Colleen. But so too were the wolves.

Noon found Dwight farther into the Badlands than he had ever before ventured in winter. Still the winding trail drew him on. Now it was slanting again to the south. He understood this. Those two killers had tasted mutton and found it good, and they had no intention of being cut off from their only supply of food. Here they would stay, and kill, until the spring thaw let them retreat back to Canada.

And still the dog's trail clung stubbornly to that of the wolves. This long, winding scar that twisted and turned between the sculptured drifts was the only mark on the white mantle that covered the ground. Except for this sign of wild, savage life, the Badlands looked more than ever like part of a cold and lifeless moon.

Dwight reined in suddenly and leaned out of the saddle, frowning.

Here, for some reason, the dog had given up the chase. Dwight took off a mitten and dug his watch out from under his coats and sweaters.

"Two o'clock," he murmured. "He's been on the go for a long time—at least all night and all of today. He's tired and hungry."

The dog had turned straight south. If he kept on as he had started, he would come out somewhere between the Jerome ranch and Bucky Turnbull's. Neither Mr. Jerome nor Bucky had Dwight's proof that wolves had killed the Jerome sheep last night. He felt slightly sick as he thought of either of them drawing a bead on the dog with a gun.

"Come on, Colleen," he said.

He turned Limpy. The hound fought the chain, wanting to plunge on after the wolves, but the little pinto was glad to drag back toward home. In a few moments, Colleen gave up. She trotted wearily along beside Limpy, tongue out.

Dwight turned her loose then, and let her run. She raced on ahead, and several times he had to whistle her back.

An hour passed.

The sun was well down toward the evening horizon now. The chill had deepened. Dwight suddenly realized how tired and cold and hungry he was. He had been in the saddle almost ten hours without food.

Ahead of him, Colleen had stopped on the brow of a long slope. Her head was flung up, and her tensely stretched body no longer looked tired. Something about her sent a thrill of warning through Dwight. He put his fingers in his mouth and whistled sharply.

She paid no attention to him. He shouted, "Colleen, Colleen!" and dug his heels into the pinto's side as the hound disappeared down the slope, running hard.

Dwight reached the place where she had stopped. He reined in.

"Jeepers!" he breathed.

Down there, less than a quarter of a mile away, stood the big outlaw mutt. He was bigger, even, than Dwight remembered. He was trotting along slowly, with his nose to the ground.

Colleen paid no attention to him. She was hurling herself down the slope to the left, harder than Dwight had ever seen her run. Later, when he would tell people that he had paced off those jumps of hers, people would shake their heads doubtfully. No dog, they said, could run in thirty-foot leaps. But Colleen had.

Suddenly Dwight saw the wolves.

One moment there was nothing. The next, there were those two lean, gray shapes gliding silently over the snow. Dwight went cold all over.

One moment there was no sound at all in this dead, white, moonlike world. The next, Colleen had burst into a full-throated, half-crazed baying— a bell-like hound sound Dwight had never heard from her before.

The big mutt looked up. His deep, resonant voice joined in. As he raced to join Colleen, Dwight understood.

The dog had not quit the chase at all. He was smart! He had simply taken a chance that the wolves would circle back to where he had first picked up their trail this morning, north of the Jerome ranch. He had cut across the country the short way, letting the wolves waste their strength on useless circling and twisting and crisscrossing. It took a smart dog, with strong natural hunter's instinct, to do that.

"Colleen!" Dwight shouted again, and there was as much admiration as fear in his voice.

The wolfhound was bred for the show ring, but no one had to tell her what to do now. She had never hunted real wolves. She had never hunted with another dog, and she had never seen this big mutt before.

Yet, instead of going to his side, she made straight for the wolves, counting on the big mutt to attack from his side. They worked as a team, instinct responding to instinct. Their frenzied, bell-like baying made the two wolves cringe to the snow . . . made Dwight forget cold and hunger and weariness. He shrieked encouragement and wrestled with his plunging horse and tried to get the Arisaka rifle out of its boot.

Yet if the two dogs could hunt as a team, so could the wolves. It was as though a signal passed between them. The big mutt was by far the closer. The she-wolf, still crouching with her belly in the snow, went gliding off to one side. Her mate sprang to meet the big mutt. They closed in mid-air. The she-wolf came in below them, slashing up from the side.

The big dog made no sound as they struck him.

There was something grim and chilling about the terrible silence of those first few split seconds after the dog and the he-wolf met, jaw to jaw.

Then Colleen was on them, still baying, now slashing and tearing, throwing herself at the wolves with a fury Dwight had never thought her capable of.

Limpy had the wolf scent in his nostrils and would not stand. Dwight looped the reins around his arm and slid out of the saddle. He leveled the gun, but the two wolves and the two dogs were locked in one threshing, twisting tangle that rolled over and over and over in the snow. He dared not shoot.

Suddenly the big mutt reared up on his hind legs. He had one of the wolves by the flank. It twisted and screamed and snapped at his belly as he shook its seventy half-starved pounds.

Down they came, and the fight was suddenly over. The two gray forms went streaking across the snow in full retreat. The big mutt tried to follow, but he had been clearly hurt.

Dwight, his heart in his throat, whistled at Colleen. She would have followed the wolves, which stopped after a little way, waiting for her to come within reach. They would take one more chance to kill one lone dog between them, having disabled the big mutt.

Colleen sensed danger. She turned back at his whistle.

Dwight leveled the Arisaka and fired. It was too

far to hope to hit anything. The wolves flinched at the sound . . . and were gone.

Dwight jacked another load into the gun and looked around for the big mutt.

The dog too was gone. In a moment Dwight saw him running steadily toward the southwest. He had a bad limp, but was covering ground swiftly. Dwight shook his head in pity.

"Gun shy, I guess," he murmured. "Guess he learned all he wants to know about rifles from Walt Trescoli."

It was hard to frighten Dwight, yet he was glad to get back into the saddle. He had heard stories of men being cornered on the ground by wolves. He rode several miles before getting off to examine Colleen.

The hound had only a few small wounds, for the big mutt had taken most of the punishment.

It was well after dark when a tired boy on a tired horse reached home, with a still more tired dog shambling along behind, head down, tail dragging.

A strange dog—a white collie with a black spot over his right eye—came out of the sheepshed to warn them away. Dwight's father had lost no time in getting a dog to replace the dead Feistie and Wrangle. Colleen snarled at the new dog and went on up to the house.

Mr. Jerome came out from behind the sheepshed, carrying a shovel.

"How about giving me a hand, Dwight?" he asked.

Dwight dreaded these times, because his father was always so deeply hurt. He went back of the sheepshed. There his father had scooped aside the snow and hacked a hole into the frozen ground with a pick. Other men might just throw dead dogs into a ditch somewhere, but Clayton Jerome would spend all day cutting an honorable grave in the wintry ground.

Feistie and Wrangle lay beside the hole. The father knelt between them a moment, with a hand on each.

"Poor old dogs!" he said. "Poor old dogs!"

"You go on up and feed Limpy, Dad," said Dwight. "Let me take care of this."

His father was crying as he walked away, leading the pinto. Dwight buried the two dogs without tears. He was sad, but his mind was too full of the vivid, brutal death fight he had seen just a few hours before.

His father listened in silence as Dwight told him what he had seen.

"That's bad," Mr. Jerome said at the end, "because if there are two wolves, there could easily be twenty, or a hundred. Still, we know it wasn't wolves at Bucky's place, and at Jake's. We've got *both* wolves and a sheep-killing dog, and I wish I knew which was worse."

Dwight shook his head. The term sheep-killing dog called to mind the picture of a skulking, furtive killer who led a double life. By day such a killer was someone's pet, as a rule. By night he was a murderer who killed, not for food, but for the cruel pleasure of killing.

And Dwight knew deeply that the big mutt simply did not fit this picture. True, he had killed sheep, but he had done it boldly, once in broad daylight. He had fought wolves, hunting them down tirelessly, outsmarting them, and in the end closing in that thrilling, never-to-be-forgotten battle in the snow.

"Dad, he's not that kind of killer," Dwight said earnestly. "He's a good dog. I just don't think he knows any better."

"It doesn't make much difference whether he knows better or not. The damage is done when the first sheep is killed. Dwight, don't let's get soft-hearted now, over a sheep killer."

Dwight, who had just seen his father cry over two dead dogs, found this hard to answer. Certainly his father was not like old Bucky Turnbull.

"I can tell you, he'd be the greatest wolf dog in the world," Dwight said. "And how he'll hate wolves, after they've cut him up—the way I've always wanted Colleen to hate them."

Mr. Jerome shook his head. "Once a sheep killer, always a sheep killer, Son. When they get the taste of blood, they're through. They seem to go crazy, and I've never heard of a sheep killer who could be cured."

"This one could be," said Dwight. "If you'd only

seen him stand up and fight! It didn't matter much
to him whether he lived or not, just so he got his
grip. Let me catch him and bring him home."

The man threw his arm around the boy.
"Dwight, all I know is raising sheep, and I suppose
you'll end up as a sheepman too. It's not much of a
life, but I like it. I like my neighbors too. And a
sheepman's first duty is to his sheep, and his neighbors' sheep. You don't think we could bring home
the dog that killed Bucky's and Jake's sheep, do
you?"

Dwight's shoulders slumped. "No, I guess not.
But—"

"You're a sheepman's son. You're a sheepman
yourself, and a good one. Not everything in this
world is fair and pleasant, or just the way we want
it. When you find yourself feeling sorry for the
dog, try to think of the poor, defenseless sheep
instead. Now, go clean your gun and get some
supper and go to bed. You've had a hard day."

"All right," Dwight said. He was suddenly weary in every muscle. "I am kind of tired and hungry, at that."

For the first time in months, Dwight slept late
the next morning. He was awakened by the voice
of Joe Turnbull, out in the yard. He dressed,
swarmed down the ladder, and ran outside.

Dwight and Joe had been friends since small
boyhood. They were not much alike, as friends go,
for Joe cared little for riding and hunting. A little

older, taller, and heavier than Dwight, Joe was chiefly interested in baseball. His father had played professional ball, and had once tried out with a major league team. Joe had one ruling ambition— someday to pitch a world series game. His father had worked with him ever since Joe was big enough to hold a baseball.

Dwight, who had felt the power of his friend's fast one through a well-padded mitt, had no doubt that Joe would get what he wanted. For his part, Joe believed Dwight to be the greatest hunter and rider in the Northwest.

"About time you're up," Mr. Jerome said. "Joe's going to help you. I'll get Limpy ready while you're eating."

"Help me what?"

"Run that big dog down. Joe says the county commissioners will offer a reward for him today. If you look sharp, you boys can earn next year's school clothes before schools open next week."

Dwight threw his friend an unhappy glance.

"That's right," Joe said soberly.

Neighbors. A sheepman's duty was to his neighbors. . . .

"All right," Dwight said. "I'll be right out."

He kept his feelings to himself. He knew the big mutt was wounded. To be driven off from the only food he knew, after his game fight against the wolves—it wasn't fair!

Colleen was eager for a run. The two boys held their horses to a slow canter as they followed her.

It was the father's idea that they search the Badlands. Dwight agreed with relief, feeling sure in his own mind that, though they might meet wolves, they never would see the dog where they would search today.

No, the dog was holed up somewhere else.

"It would be pretty easy to get lost out here," Joe said uneasily, as the house faded from view.

Dwight laughed. "Ah, I could go home blindfolded!"

Joe grinned. "You just get home with your eyes open. That's all I expect from you."

They ranged the Badlands widely. They saw plenty of tracks, mostly of coyotes, and once they came across the unmistakable long-clawed sign of a big Saskatchewan cruiser. They tried to follow it, but the wily old wolf's trail showed he expected to be followed. He circled, twisted, zigzagged, and crossed coyote tracks endlessly, with his endless patience wearing down theirs.

When they came home that night, Dwight's father was gone. A few telephone lines had been repaired, among them their own. Mr. Jerome was a township supervisor, and all the supervisors had been called in tonight to meet with the county commissioners.

He came home late that evening. A big crowd had attended the meeting, he reported. A reward of five hundred dollars was offered for the dog, two hundred for each Canadian wolf.

"That's putting it backward," Dwight said.

"Maybe," his father sighed, "but you can't argue with folks. Feeling is pretty high. No one but you has seen any wolves, and everybody has seen this dog . . . or at least they think they have."

For a week Dwight and Joe roamed the Badlands. Dwight felt guilty, because he had long since made up his mind that the big mutt was holed up south of the highway somewhere. But if people wanted him to search the Badlands—why, all right, he'd search the Badlands!

School opened again the following Monday. Once more the trains were running, although some roads were still closed, and a few would not be opened until the spring thaw.

Dwight found it pleasant in the warm schoolroom, with the lignite blazing hotly in the two cherry-red stoves, and Miss Stevenson's pretty, dark head bent over her book or her laughing voice leading a class through its lesson. Miss Stevenson was seeing a lot of Deputy Bill Ehmken. She didn't mind being teased about it, either. She seemed to laugh quite a lot lately. . . .

But Dwight's mind was on the big mutt.

"The three branches of government are the executive, represented by the President and his cabinet, the legislative, represented by the Congress, and the judicial, represented by the Supreme Court and the inferior Federal courts."

Where is the outlaw holed up?

"The Supreme Court is composed of eight Associate Justices and one Chief Justice, who presides.

They serve for life or until voluntary retirement, unless impeached. They are appointed by the President with the consent of the Senate. This is considered the best example of the American Constitutional system of checks and balances."

Maybe he's dead. Maybe those wolves cut him up so badly that he just crawled off and died.

"The Congress is composed of the Senate and the House of Representatives. . . ."

Maybe he's left the country. Or maybe the people who lost him have found him again. I hope so.

"Dwight," said Miss Stevenson, "I'm afraid you aren't paying attention. You've got an examination to pass to get into your sophomore class next year, you know. Now define the duties of the Vice-President."

"Yes, ma'am. I'm sorry."

He'd be mine if I caught him. Their phone didn't answer when Sheriff Lang called. . . .

Part of Dwight kept roaming the Badlands, the gullied country south of the highway, peering into every den and hole and burrow, looking for a big, wounded dog he knew was not all bad.

And the dog wasn't. He just didn't know any better. Dwight could not say how he knew this. He just knew it. . . .

CHAPTER SEVEN

TEN DAYS LATER THE BIG MUTT STRUCK AGAIN. This time it was at the Phil Quist place, ten miles from the Jeromes' and, for the first time, south of the highway. The morning light showed the dog's tracks plainly.

When Deputy Bill came out to investigate he shook his head gravely. There were two dead sheep, and one of them was Phil Quist's high-priced Southdown ram.

The Quists were newly married. They were ambitious. They had hoped to have a purebred Southdown flock in a few years. They had gone without curtains for their windows and rugs for their floors to buy the ram. Now it might be many years before they could have curtains and rugs.

"It's started," said Bill. "First they kill one, and pretty soon it's a dozen. Didn't you hear anything?"

"Yes," said Mrs. Quist. "The dogs made a little fuss once, and woke me up."

"Where were they?"

"In the house."

"Sheep dogs belong with the sheep," said Bill.

"See, this rascal came up to your kitchen door and made himself right at home. From the looks of his tracks, he stayed here a long time. . . ."

Bill Ehmken was wrong. It was a sick, lonesome dog, not a savage, bloodthirsty one, that had made himself at home at the Quist place and broken the Quists' hearts.

Nearly a week the outlaw mutt lay in his den, after Walt Trescoli's bullet furrowed its way through the flesh of his leg. Now there was no woman to baby his hurts, and cluck and coo and cry over him. But the dog's instinct served him even better. It told him what to do when he became sick and feverish from his wounds.

They were not dangerous wounds, but his skin had been ripped in several places. The worst was a long gash in his belly, where the she-wolf had slashed him as he shook her. But even here, the strong muscles were undamaged. So he lay quietly, hour on hour, not eating, moving only a little. Now and then he crawled to the door and gulped snow, to cool his feverish body.

Fresh air, which came down the ventilating tunnel, and plenty of rest—these healed him. He became gaunt and bony, but still he lay there and let his sick body rest.

Several times the coyotes came back and lurked at the doorway to the den. They whined complainingly in their shrill, peevish voices. Perhaps he had brought home some of the wolf smell, to tell them what had happened.

But they knew he was not yet weak and sick enough for them to attack. Each time, the coyotes trotted back to their makeshift den in the straw-stack. They too were gaunt and hungry, ready to take risks. Had the dog been just a little weaker, had the wolves slashed him a little deeper, they might have challenged him for the den.

In a few days, the fever was gone. He no longer craved snow. He was weak, but not sick. Somehow he knew it was time to stop resting his huge, empty body, and feed it.

He came out at nightfall, and luck was with him. As he came clambering stiffly out of the gully, two jack rabbits jumped up in front of him. He snapped at one. Its wild leap carried it back-ward, over the edge into the deep snow down in the gully. The other followed blindly.

The dog caught them easily and carried them back into his den. Their warm flesh brought his strength back quickly.

Still he rested. The next day he came out again. Limping along through the gullied land south of the highway, he came upon two coyotes feeding on a newly killed calf. They had found it in a snow-bank where it had somehow survived, although barely living. He drove the coyotes away, but when he returned later that evening he found nothing but polished bones.

That night he deliberately hunted sheep. Still, it was not their scent, but that of some food the Quists had thrown out for their dogs, that drew the

outlaw there. The Quists' dogs were too well fed. They had left most of these table scraps when they went into the house to sleep behind the stove.

The dog stood sniffing at the frozen scraps for a long time. The moon was rising, and by now he knew the danger that lurked around these little ranches. Still he lingered, perhaps wishing that he too could be overfed, and sleep in a warm house once more.

The mutt had changed much. He had learned to carry his tail differently, lower down, as a balance and rudder. When he ran, he no longer had the clumsy, bouncing gait of a fat city dog playing on a vacant lot. There was a gliding smoothness to his movements that was much like the gait of the wolves. As he stood nosing the pile of food frozen in the snow, there was an alertness that showed in every line of his body.

Inside the Quist house a dog stood up, yawned, and turned around sleepily before lying down again. The big mutt's keen ears caught the sound. He took a step toward the house, and then another. He whined softly. At the kitchen door, he put his nose down to the crack and pulled a long, noisy breath. In a moment he lay down, his nose to a rush of warm air that came out through the crack.

For a long time he lay there, not daring to whine, not daring to scratch to be let in. His tail moved softly over the rough pine boards of the porch.

Then a sheep moved noisily down in the shed, and the dog's huge hunger returned.

His big head was clearly outlined against the sky as he put his forefeet on the top of the corral fence. Had Phil Quist awakened then—

But he did not, and the dog went over the fence silently. He had learned the ways of sheep. He knew their tendency to pile on top of each other, in their stupid search for a hiding place. It was not necessary to startle the whole flock.

Coolly he selected a fat young ewe. She made no sound as he struck her down. It was done so quietly that the other sheep, instead of climbing on top of each other, only gave a small, restless surge. Quickly they were calm again.

The dog dragged his kill to the other end of the shed. A big ram came stalking out of the flock, shaking his head. His dull mind had suddenly grasped the fact that something was wrong. He put his head down blindly, and charged.

The dog stepped aside. Once more the ram charged. Once more the dog stepped nimbly out of his way, but this time he growled a warning.

The growl only infuriated the ram. A third time he charged. The dog's deepest nature was to defend his kill. One slash . . . and Phil Quist's high-priced ram stumbled a few steps, and fell down.

The dog had only done the thing bred into him by nature and mankind, but this would be small comfort to Phil Quist tomorrow. Afterward, the dog leaped the fence and ran again to the pile of frozen table scraps. He whined in his throat, and his shaggy tail waved. Once more he crept to the kitchen door and lay there, snuffling at the crack under the door.

One of the lazy sheep dogs sat up and made a little gruff barking noise. He trotted into the kitchen.

"What's the matter, Tango—bad dream?" a woman said sleepily. "Go to bed and be quiet!"

The outlaw was already loping for home. Stronger than his craving for human companionship was his fear of guns. He forgot both his wounds and his loneliness in his eagerness to hide.

He found that the five coyotes had moved back into the den during his absence. In a bad temper, he scattered them savagely, crawled in, and went to sleep.

Shortly after noon, Dwight heard a car stop in the schoolyard. He knew the sound of that engine, and so did most of the other boys. Miss Stevenson turned pink at their chuckles.

"Let's be quiet, please," she said primly.

When Deputy Bill came in, he was not smiling. He talked in a low voice with the teacher for several minutes. She turned toward Dwight.

"Dwight, will you come here a moment, please?"

Dwight put down his book and came forward. "Hello, Bill."

"Hello, Dwight. Your dad tells me you got two

good looks at this big dog, once in the car and once out there in the Badlands. Would you know him if you saw him again?"

"Would I!"

"Even at a distance?"

"I'd know him as far as I could see him," Dwight said positively.

"Where do you think he ranges?"

"Not far from here. He's got a den down below the highway somewhere, I think. Why?"

Dwight swelled a little. When Bill Ehmken came to him for advice—well, that was something! But he thought with pity of the big outlaw. He wouldn't last long, with Bill after him.

"I just left your dad," Bill said. "He says it's all right for you to skip school for a few days. Let's get this scamp, Dwight, before he does any more damage. What do you say?"

Dwight looked out of the window, his spirits falling.

More than anything else in the world, he wanted to be out with Bill Ehmken, the Arisaka under his arm and Limpy fighting the bit and wanting to run. Just the two of them—no books, no school, no regular mealtimes, nothing to do but hunt. Only the darkness to send them home, and not even then, if they chose to stay out.

But the thought of seeing the dog go down from a bullet made him suddenly sick and white. He bit his lip and shook his head. "I don't think I want to, Bill."

"Why not, Dwight?" Miss Stevenson asked, as Bill remained silent.

Dwight looked at her, hoping she'd understand even if Bill didn't. "Because he isn't vicious," he pleaded. "He's just an old fool dog that doesn't know any better."

"I'm afraid you're wrong," said Bill. He told Dwight about Phil Quist's sheep. "Two of them, this time. The dog's tracks are as plain as day. It's not a question of just a playful dog any longer. He's got the taste of blood."

The rest of the pupils could overhear what Bill was saying in his deep voice. They were sheepmen's children. Dwight knew what they'd be saying about him tomorrow.

Still he shook his head. "Please! I don't want to, Bill. He's a wolf killer, not a sheep killer. I don't know what happened, but it can't be the way you think."

"You prove I'm wrong, Dwight, and I'll buy you the best saddle in the catalogue."

Miss Stevenson patted Dwight's shoulder. "Think of it this way, Dwight. It's not pleasant, when you love dogs so. But not all duty is pleasant. I couldn't do what they want you to do. No one else could. Don't you see that it's up to you? You've never backed down yet, have you? Your own people are counting on you."

Bill put his hand out. "Here, Dwight. You put me on that dog's trail, and this is yours to keep."

It was Bill's Distinguished Service Cross, won on

Okinawa at the time he got that wound from the Arisaka he had brought home to Dwight. Dwight looked up, meeting Bill's eyes steadily. Bill had earned that medal by doing his duty, plus a little more. It probably hadn't been much fun for him, either. Bill was not smiling now. Bill understood.

"All right, Bill," Dwight said. "I'll go."

"Then get your lunch pail and coat. We might as well start now, from the Quists', while we've got a place to start from."

For five days they hunted together.

Again and again, they crossed the big dog's sign. But he had become an expert evader. There was, in fact, too much sign. Like the wolves, he had learned to double back on his own trail, to jump and circle and crisscross. Sooner or later, all trails came down to the bare, paved highway, where the snowplows had long since made tracking impossible.

"I give up," said Bill. "I've never been fooled so badly in my life. Dwight, I guess you might as well go back to school. We're wasting time."

They were sitting in the sheriff's warm office in the courthouse. It was evening, and they had been out since daylight. Dwight was dozing by the big stove. The sheriff's next words brought him wide awake.

"No, keep on hunting," the old man said. "Let me try one thing more. I've got a fellow coming from Minneapolis tomorrow with a pair of bloodhounds. They've never tracked a dog, but he claims they can, and will, trail anything."

Dwight had heard of bloodhounds, but he had never seen one before. Their appearance, when they arrived, surprised and delighted him. They were big, affectionate, sad-eyed creatures who took an instant liking to him when they were let out of the car on the highway. Their owner and Dwight quickly became friends. This pair of dogs, the man said, was worth a thousand dollars. These were famous trackers which had already won fame by their work in criminal cases.

It was uncanny how quickly the hounds learned what was expected of them. There was no question in Dwight's mind but that they were tracking the outlaw. His heart fell as he watched them race across the snow, sounding their deep, ringing voices. Soon, however, they came to the highway. Here they lost the scent.

Again and again they were brought back; again and again they stopped at the same dead end of bare pavement.

"Too many conflicting scents. Too many coyotes and cars and other dogs," the sheriff said gloomily.

The bloodhounds were taken back to Minneapolis, and for another week nothing was heard of the dog.

The outlaw had heard the bloodhounds. He did not have to be told what they were tracking. He heard the voices of the men, as he lay in his stolen den. When evening came, he slipped out and ran swiftly. He did not come back until the bloodhounds were long since gone, and even their memory had faded from his mind.

He had not merely been frightened away. He had learned to catch jack rabbits, and while they were seeking him down by the highway, on trails which hourly grew colder, he was having a fine frolic up in the Badlands.

His wounds were all healed. He had grown lean and tough and nimble and fast. He learned quickly—learned how jacks, when they're tiring, turn suddenly and run back between a dog's legs, startling him and sometimes tripping him. The first time this happened, the rabbit got away while the big mutt was picking himself up out of the snow. The next time, there was a yelp, a click of teeth, a squeal—and the rabbit was flung high into the air with a broken back.

The mutt soon tired of this. A few days' warm weather had made it possible for him to find shelter wherever the night found him. One evening the wind rose and the temperature fell. The dog remembered his warm, protected den down in the deep, sheltered gully. Like a lost dog going home, he returned to it.

Once again the coyotes had moved in; once again he drove them out.

That night, he added insult to injury by killing one of Bucky Turnbull's sheep. He stopped on his way out to nose around Bucky's yard, where no dog was ever allowed. He left a maze of tracks which sent the old bachelor to the telephone for a long, angry conversation with the sheriff.

With Deputy Bill, Dwight visited Bucky's place and examined the ground. He hardened his heart against the big dog when he saw the dead sheep, the unmistakable tracks in the snow. Bucky was furious. He threatened to fire on every dog he saw. Glumly Dwight went back with Bill to town.

"What next?" said Bill. "Got any ideas, Dwight?"

Dwight shook his head.

"We could try a wolf drag," the sheriff suggested.

Wolf drags were used whenever the coyote population became so numerous as to cause trouble to the sheepmen. Hundreds of men formed as big a square as they could cover with their guns. Sometimes five or six square miles were enclosed this way. They started marching toward the center, shouting, beating the bushes, stopping only to smoke out holes and burrows where coyotes might hide. Behind the lines rode the best marksmen, to run down and shoot coyotes which managed to slip through.

Bill thought this over.

"Let me try one more thing first, Cecil," he said to the sheriff. "A drag won't do any good unless we know where to drag. Let me rent a plane and take Dwight up, and see if we can't figure out where this dog hides out."

"Me?" Dwight cried. "In an airplane?"

He had never flown before, and for a while, at least, he was able to forget his feeling of deep guilt about the dog.

For it had become a real feeling of guilt. Riding with Bill, following the bloodhounds, ransacking every nook and cranny where the dog might be hiding, he had been silent and unhappy. Even the killing at Bucky's place did not shock him for long. He knew it was wrong to kill sheep, but deep in his heart he pitied the dog. Over and over his thoughts ran: *What else could the dog do? What else could he do?*

Men hated a sheep-killing dog worse than they hated a wolf, because they regarded it as a traitor, repaying man's kindness with ingratitude and treachery. But who had been kind to the outlaw, Dwight wondered. What did he owe the sheepmen— or any man, for that matter? There was small chance that he had been lost out of the New York car. No, those people had abandoned him.

"What else could he do?" Dwight asked himself again and again. "They're the ones who ought to have to pay."

Early one morning a small, four-place cabin plane flew in from Bismarck. It landed in the Jeromes' level barley field south of the highway, and Dwight's father held his breath as it swayed and teetered and roared over the ground between the drifts, taking the air. Dwight saw his father's worried face flash past under the ship, and then he and Bill were air-borne, and the wild part of him thrilled to the birdlike wildness of flight.

Bill leaned close to his ear. "I thought if we got up here and got a look at things, where we could see everything at once, maybe you could figure out where he's hidden out. Watch carefully, Dwight. Tell me where you want to go, and we'll go there."

Dwight looked out. At first it was all strange, but in a little while he began to recognize ranches and roads and other landmarks. He frowned and motioned to be taken back, and the pilot wheeled the plane and they came back along the route of the highway.

"See anything yet?" Bill shouted.

"I'm not sure," Dwight answered.

Again they turned and roared back over the highway. Nothing moved down there, but Dwight had a sudden, tingling sense of having come close to something. Once more he signaled; once more the pilot turned.

This had been a good idea of Bill's! There were the Badlands, there was Bucky's place, and Phil Quist's and Vaughn Jacobs', and his father's. It was somehow like a big, invisible wheel, with spokes radiating out from a hub that lay in the rough, gullied land south of the highway. There lay the center of everything—and there, too, was the bare stretch of pavement where all trails had ended.

Dwight pointed down. "Down there somewhere, Bill, in one of those deep draws—that's where he's denned up."

"What makes you think so?"

"I don't know. A city dog would stick close to the pavement, wouldn't he?"

"Maybe."

"And that's the center of everything. I mean— well, I don't know how to explain it, but that's where I'd hide if it was me."

Bill tapped the pilot on the shoulder, and in a few minutes they were crunching over the snow-covered barley stubble.

It was too late to hunt that day, but early the next morning they were out. Bill had spent the night at the Jerome place. He rode Mr. Jerome's bay Sparrow while Dwight rode Limpy.

They went straight to the long stretch of bare pavement. Here they turned south and began riding along parallel to the highway. Again Dwight felt that tingling sensation, and his heart filled with dread.

Bill pulled in and pointed to the snow ahead of him.

"See? You were right again. There's where all of his trails come together," he said.

There was no mistake. The dog wisely had never left the pavement at the same point twice, leaving no mark over the crusted snow. Yet as he neared the deep gully he had worn one path that stood out sharp and clear.

Bill slid his rifle quietly out of its boot. He dropped to the ground and handed his reins up to Dwight. He patted Dwight's leg.

"Turn your back if you want to, boy. I think this time we've got him cornered. I know how you feel, and I don't blame you a bit."

Dwight tried to turn his back, but found himself frozen.

The big dog, sleeping in his den, heard the thud of hoofs over his head. He shot out of his den and clawed his way up the bank. Bill stood staring, too amazed to lift his gun as the dog brushed past him. The horses reared. Dwight let out a long, shrill cry.

By the time Bill could get the gun to his shoulder, the dog was out of range in rough country where the horses could not hope to follow. Ruefully, Bill fired three shots after him anyway.

"To wish him a happy trip," he said. "Well, anyway we know where he lives."

Dwight swallowed his pleasure, which seemed about to turn to tears. He shook his head. "Not for a while. He won't come back here soon, after a scare like that."

"Then at least we're rid of him."

Some of the color had come back into Dwight's face. He thought, *I wouldn't ever want to speak to Bill again, if he had killed him.* He looked down at the ground.

"No, he'll be back. Not to this den, because he's learned his lesson, but back to this country. He

97

likes it here. That's what I've been telling you, Bill. He's just a fool dog that's lonesome and lost and hungry, and doesn't know any better. When he gets real hungry, he'll want a home again. I wish you'd give me a chance to show you."

"I wish I could let you," said Bill. "Maybe this will help square things."

He dropped something into Dwight's hand. It was his D.S.C. Dwight tried to hand it back.

"We didn't get him, Bill, and I don't want it anyway."

"Keep it," said Bill. "I didn't say we had to get him. I just said to put me on his trail, and you did. I guess what you've done is over and above the call of duty, son."

Dwight dropped the medal into his pocket. It was hard to stay mad at Bill.

That night, reporting to Sheriff Lang, the big deputy said: "Cecil, Clay Jerome's wrong when he calls that kid half wild. He's not half—he's *all* wild. And it's too bad he can't have his way. He'd make a good dog of that outlaw."

"You can't reform a sheep killer," said the sheriff.

"That's what I thought, and it's wrong. Dwight could. Listen, that kid can do things with an animal that no other person in the world could do. It was uncanny, watching his face in that place. He wasn't guessing. I tell you, he *knew* where that dog was. If he knew that, he knows enough to break it of sheep-killing."

"Bill," the sheriff said, "there's no use arguing. There's not a sheepman in the country who would stand for it. His own dad wouldn't let him keep a sheep killer a single night."

"I guess so," Bill sighed. "This is going to break that boy's heart, though. Because we'll get that big scamp. Maybe not tomorrow, maybe not the next day, but soon. We've got him on the run now."

CHAPTER EIGHT

UP IN THE BADLANDS a lean wolf sat down, pointed his nose at the waning moon, and howled.

His mate had run on ahead of him. She turned at his howl, sat down in the snow, and waited for him to catch up with her. All night they had prowled restlessly, much of the time in plain sight of the dark huddle of buildings that was the Jerome ranch. The scent of sheep came clearly, pulling the she-wolf on and on and on. Just as clear, though, was the scent of danger, which held her mate back.

But if he was lean, she was leaner still, and hungrier, and more ready to take a chance. In a moment she got up impatiently and trotted on without him. He followed when he saw she would not wait.

Bucky Turnbull was just getting out of bed when he heard that howl. It came from close by—over near the Jerome place, he guessed. His telephone line had been repaired and he called Sheriff Lang at once. The old officer answered sleepily.

"Hello, Sheriff Lang speaking."

"Cecil, I just heard that sheep-killing dog howling, over in the Badlands north of Clay Jerome's. What good's a wolf drag down there below the highway, if it's up here? You're just wasting a whole day for everybody! I've got a notion not to go."

"How do you know it was a dog?" Sleepy as he was, the sheriff knew that Bucky was in one of his worst tempers. He tried to soothe the angry little man. "Maybe it was a wolf."

"Wolf! That's just Clay Jerome's crazy talk," Bucky snapped. "Who else saw any wolves, besides that Jerome kid? They're all in his imagination, and I'm staying home today."

"We're doing the best we can, Bucky, and I wish you'd come along. We need every man we can get."

"Well . . . all right. But we better get some results."

All over the county, alarm clocks had been set, guns cleaned and oiled, lunches packed. Clayton Jerome was just getting up when he heard that howl, but he knew what it was. He went to the door and whistled, and Patch's bark answered him, telling him that everything was still all right down at the sheepshed.

But Mr. Jerome was still uneasy. He pushed Colleen outside.

"Out you go! You can sleep in the coalpit. It's about time you started to earn your keep, old girl."

It was just four o'clock when he closed the door and called softly up the ladder to the attic: "All hunters out, all hunters out! While the hunters sleep, the game gets away. Come on, boys—time to rise."

Joe Turnbull had spent the night with Dwight, and would ride Sparrow in the wolf drag today. The boys had lain awake late, arguing about the dog. Dwight had tried to put into words the way he felt about the big mutt. He hated a sheep killer as bad as the next man. He knew that wolf drags were necessary, now and then.

But he remembered that fight between the dog and the wolves, which he alone had seen. If only he could make people understand! The sight of the big mutt springing to the attack was one never to be forgotten. A cowardly sheep killer just didn't fight that way.

Remembering this, the wolf drag seemed a monstrous injustice. He tried to tell Joe about it, but Joe was shocked to hear defense of a sheep-killing dog. They almost quarreled.

"You'd better not let Uncle Bucky hear you talk that way," Joe warned. "He hates dogs anyway."

"I don't care who hears," Dwight said. "This dog's *not* that kind of sheep killer."

"He killed sheep, didn't he?"

"But not the way you think."

"All right, he's not a sheep killer—but he's five hundred dollars. Someone's going to get that bounty money. Why not us?"

"I wouldn't touch a cent of it."

Dwight dreaded the morning. When his father called them in the morning, he turned over and stared out of the dark window. Joe jumped out of bed and dressed quickly.

"Hey, Dwight, are you still asleep?"

Dwight looked up at the ceiling. "I'm not going," he said.

"What you need is a good workout," said Joe, jumping on him. "Smell that ham and eggs."

Mr. Jerome came up the ladder as the two boys wrestled on the bed. "I don't know what good it does me to be quiet, the way you two are carrying on. You'll wake up everyone clear to Bismarck," he said.

He went downstairs. Joe said soberly: "Come on, Dwight. I know how you feel, but what can we do, against the whole county?"

"Nothing, I guess," Dwight said after a silence.

"You've got to go."

"I suppose so," Dwight said wearily.

He got up and dressed, went down and ate breakfast. His mother and the girls were still asleep.

Mr. Jerome left in the car. He was a line captain, and would be in charge of one side of the square today. The boys saddled Limpy and Sparrow, and waited in the yard. In a few minutes Deputy Bill came cantering in on a horse followed by five other men and boys—all good riders, all crack shots. In a few minutes, five others arrived.

They waited here, as the eastern sky gradually grew gray. It was supposed to be an honor to "back up" the line, but Dwight could not join in the horseplay of these other dead shots. He leaned against Limpy, wondering where the big dog was now. He felt sick every time he thought of him as being cornered in the drag.

Deputy Bill came over and said, "Your heart isn't in this, is it?"

"Not very much," Dwight confessed.

"Why don't you skip it? We can get along without you."

Dwight met his eyes. "How was it on Okinawa? Did they tell you they could get along without you too?"

He wished Bill wouldn't talk about it, and Bill seemed to understand. Bill walked away.

A few minutes later they swung into the saddles, and Bill gave them their orders.

"We'll have four sides to watch, and there are only twelve of us, so look sharp. I want Dwight and Joe on the north side, with me," he said. "No more horseplay from now on. Handle your guns carefully, and make your horses behave. A wild shot could kill a man. Keep your eyes open! Remember, you're shooting for five hundred dollars today."

Dwight tried the action on the Arisaka. The copper-jacketed bullets were icy to the touch. He slipped the gun back into its boot and followed Bill. Colleen came out of the coalpit, whining.

"Go back," he said.

She went down into the pit again, obeying his order. A light was just gleaming in his mother's window as they rode out of the yard.

The four lines had already formed a square, when Bill and the boys reached their position on the bare, wind-swept north slope. Here the red earth had been scoured clean, but farther down the slope, the men on foot were waiting in deep snow.

As far as the eye could see, the line of armed hunters stretched. Every man or boy who could shoulder a rifle or shotgun had turned out today, many coming great distances. There were a few with only pistols, and even some women and girls, in overalls and high boots. All carried sandwiches, although the American Legion Auxiliary would sell hot lunches down at the highway, at the end of the drag.

In addition to their guns, most men carried strong clubs, for use at the finish of the hunt. Only a few would be permitted to shoot then, when several hundred persons came together in a small, rough, brush-covered area.

Dwight's position was at the east end of the north line. The line would move southward, past Dwight's house, down to the highway, and on across it. There it would meet the other three sides

of the square, in the maze of gullies where he and
Bill had surprised the big mutt.

Sheriff Lang's car came bouncing up the slope.
He was too old to walk in the drag, or even to ride
a horse behind it. He would keep in touch with all
four sides, as best he could, from his car. He looked
at his watch.

"All set, Bill?"

"All set, boss."

"Then let's get going." The sheriff took a re-
peating shotgun from his car and fired three quick
shots into the air. A cheer went down the line,
which surged forward at a run. They would slow
down soon enough, as they reached rougher country and deeper snow.

Dwight held Limpy in, until the hunters were
well ahead of him. He began trotting slowly back
and forth behind the line. To his right rode Deputy
Bill, and beyond Bill was Joe Turnbull. To
Dwight's left, on the other line, was Walt Trescoli,
a crack shot.

Dwight's heart was sick. What chance did the
dog have? Anything that broke through the curtain
of fire laid down by the line could not hope to
escape the riders behind.

The savage wolves hunted in packs, but never
such packs as this. It was kill or be killed, eat or
starve! Nature made the rules here, and mankind
had to abide by them. Mankind must hunt in
packs, like the wolves, because sheep meant money, and money meant food. Unless these nightly

killings were stopped, they would all go hungry. So Dwight slipped the safety catch off the Arisaka and kept it under his arm. He was a sheepman's son. There was no answer to that.

The hunters were walking more slowly now, saving their breath as they floundered through drifts and stopped to poke into holes and dens and burrows. The lines grew shorter, the square became smaller. Shorter, too, were the intervals of silence between gunshots. At first no coyotes had been seen. Now suddenly they were seen everywhere, slinking furtively along ahead of the lines, disappearing, springing out suddenly, vanishing again. Dwight held his breath every time a gun was fired, but the wild yells that would have meant the death of the dog did not come.

Occasionally a coyote broke through, but most of them kept retreating, not knowing that there was no retreat. There was little to do for the riders behind the lines. Deputy Bill walked his horse along beside Dwight's for a while.

"We're getting a lot of coyotes," he said. "It's a good hunt. I've never seen them so thin, though."

"I guess so," said Dwight.

"Not much fun in this kind of hunt, is there? Look at it this way, Dwight—for every coyote killed now, we're saving five or six lambs, come lambing time. These fellows are starved, and they'll be bold as book agents by spring. But if you—"

"Sh-h-h-h!" said Dwight.

He pulled Limpy back on his haunches. Something had scurried down the ditch just ahead of him, vanishing in the deep snow and deeper brush. He knew that rich, silky, grayish fur.

Wolf!

"What's the trouble?" Bill said.

Dwight pointed with the rifle. "Down there in the ditch, Bill, a wolf—a real old cruiser. Better not let anyone get too close on foot."

"Aw!" At first Bill found it hard to believe. Then he stood up in the stirrups and shouted: "Everyone back from that draw, and keep your eyes open. Dwight saw a wolf. Stay out of the way and don't take chances. Let us handle this."

Dwight pushed Limpy forward. The little brush-filled ditch zigzagged down the slope, growing deeper and deeper, until it was a wide spring flood channel where it went under the highway bridge. Nothing moved down there now, but that tangle of brush could hide anything.

The hunt stopped, as word was passed from man to man that Dwight Jerome had seen a Saskatchewan cruiser. Few men here had ever seen one, yet the stories of their ferocity were as old as North Dakota. No one came close to the ditch as Dwight walked Limpy slowly up and down beside it.

"I see his tracks," Dwight said, peering down into the deep snow. "Let's see if we can smoke him out."

One of the trucks that followed the drag to pick

up dead coyotes had turned off the highway, which now was only a short distance away. Dwight turned to Joe.

"Go see if they've got any papers I can use for a fire," he said. "Then you'd better take Limpy up there and wait by the truck. He's going to cut up when he smells wolf."

Joe brought the papers. Dwight rode up and down the ditch, lighting wads of paper and throwing them into the brush. Limpy began dancing and fighting, and if Dwight had needed any further proof that a wolf was cornered down there, he had it now. The horse quickly became unmanageable.

Dwight dismounted and handed the reins to Joe. Once more he made sure of the Arisaka.

"I hope you know what you're doing," said Joe, as he started back toward the truck, leading Limpy.

"So do I," said Deputy Bill uneasily.

Dwight said, "So do I." He felt better now. This was a fair fight, against a killer that showed no pity, and deserved none.

With Bill behind him, he walked along beside the ditch, his eyes searching the tangle of brush, his pulse steady. It seemed queer to him that the others should be so scared and excited.

Some of his paper fires had burned out, but a few had caught the tops of the dry brush and were crackling merrily. These would keep the wolf from slipping down the ditch through the deeper brush.

It had only one way out, toward him. Except for the cheerful crackling of the fire, all was silent.

Something moved just as silently, and Dwight saw the rich, gray shagginess of the wolf. It was only a flash, but he lifted the gun to his shoulder and caught the flash in the sights and pulled the trigger.

The wolf gave a yelp of agony. It went up on its hind legs and twisted sidewise, biting at the bullet wound in its ribs. Behind Dwight, Deputy Bill fired, and Dwight saw the wolf's head jerk as the slug smashed through it. It dropped into the snow, twitching.

"Nice shot, Dwight," said Bill. "I didn't even see it."

"Nice shot yourself," said Dwight.

He reloaded and stood looking down at the dead wolf. Its narrow, slanting eyes were closed forever. Its long, cruel teeth had made their last kill. Not just a few lambs, but perhaps dozens of valuable market sheep had been saved.

The hunters had started to move on. Dwight remembered something.

"Wait a minute. That's a she-wolf. Dad says you'll sometimes find a male alone, but never a female. There's probably another one down there below."

"Hold it!" Bill shouted. "Dwight thinks there's another one down there."

Again the hunt stopped, while Dwight and Bill slowly patrolled the ditch. Dwight's fires had all gone out now, but the smoke scent would keep the wolf from going up the draw.

They reached the highway and walked out over the bridge. They leaned on the railing and looked down. Here the brush was as high as Dwight's head, the snow deep. Men would have to walk through that brush, to keep coyotes from using the draw as an escape route. Not many men were bold enough to take that chance.

"You keep a watch up here, Bill. I'm going in after him."

"Oh, no, you're not!" Bill cried.

But Dwight had already dropped over the bridge railing. It was not more than ten feet to the bottom, and the snow cushioned his fall.

Almost at once he saw the second wolf's tracks. It had been running hard down the draw, terrified by the guns. Here something—Dwight would never know what—had made it double in its tracks. It had gone back up the draw on its belly. The zigzag draw turned a corner, and he could not see what lay beyond.

"Anything down there?" Bill called.

"His tracks. He's in front of me somewhere. Stay out, Bill. There's only room for one."

"You'd better get out of there. You crazy kid, you could be killed."

"I'm all right. Just keep out of my way."

Dwight walked forward, hearing Bill warn everyone loudly: "Give him room. I don't want him to worry about hitting someone when he shoots."

Hours seemed to pass with each second. Dwight reached the corner. He put the gun barrel out ahead of him and pushed the brush aside. Still the tracks led on. He turned the corner an inch at a time.

The wolf was not there. He went onward as the ditch narrowed. He heard Bill plodding up the side of the ditch behind him, and he knew he could count on Bill's gun again.

He turned another corner and there in front of him was the wolf—and beyond it, the big mutt, in the center of the ditch.

Dwight was scarcely a dozen yards from the big dog. He could see every line of his lean, hard muscles, as he crouched. He could make out his wide, intelligent eyes, his powerful fighting jaw, his odd little houndlike ears.

More than it feared the boy, the wolf feared the dog. It was poised on its toes, its hair standing on end like a cat's. Instantly, Dwight knew what had happened. The dog had been tracking this pair of killers. All three had been caught here in the drag, in the gully.

It was all mixed up—the hunter hunting the hunter. But the dog could have run. Instead, he had forgotten all about the men and their guns. Nothing mattered now but a chance to close with his ancient enemy.

Dwight saw the dog stiffen and rise. He brought

his gun to his shoulder and fired quickly, at the wolf.

It was not a clean hit. The wolf screamed and twisted, but prompt and steady came the crack of Bill's gun.

The wolf lay still.

The dog heard those guns and smelled the burning powder. He saw the wolf die. He remembered the burn and bite and sting of a bullet. He whirled.

Without thinking, Dwight said sharply, "Down!"

The dog lay down.

"What's that?" Deputy Bill called.

"Nothing," Dwight said quickly. "You stay there. I'll drag him up."

"Be careful. Sometimes they're just playing dead. You've got yourself four hundred dollars, Dwight."

Dwight approached the wolf cautiously and prodded it with his gun. It was dead, all right. He caught it by its hind foot and dragged it up to the ground. While the hunters gathered around, to exclaim over its size, Dwight watched the ditch, dreading to see the big dog come out.

"That took nerve," said Bill, "but it wasn't smart."

"I'm sorry," said Dwight.

But he wasn't.

He was sure now of what he had only sensed before. The dog was well-behaved, and trained. It had responded instantly to his command. It could be made to respond instantly to man's command again.

They carried the dead wolves to the truck while Dwight examined the ditch carefully. The dog was gone. Evidently it had slipped all the way up to the top, and by now was legging it out of sight into the Badlands. It was safe, and right now nothing else mattered.

The family of coyotes from whom the outlaw mutt had stolen his den had returned to it after he was driven away. Here they were cornered, in the exact center of the drag. Someone remembered how Dwight had smoked out his wolf. A fire was built in the opening of the den. The coyotes darted out, to be shot as they flashed up the winding path. The old he-coyote had fed his family on many a fat spring lamb, on chickens and ducks and eggs stolen from nearby ranches. Now his whole family paid for his raids.

Dwight and Joe did not stay for the last of the hunt. Necessary or not, this part they did not enjoy.

They rode down to the highway, tied their horses, and helped the Legion ladies unload their portable coffee maker and tables. By the time the hunters arrived, the tables were loaded with baked beans and chicken, and big mugs of steaming soup and coffee.

The men ate ravenously. Over and over, Dwight heard how he had "smoked out one wolf and kicked out another."

"Two hundred and twelve coyotes too," the sheriff said. "That's pretty good."

"You're forgetting something, aren't you?" Bill asked. "The big dog. Didn't anyone see him at all?"

Dwight felt Joe nudge him in the silence that followed.

"You did, didn't you?" Joe whispered.

Dwight flushed with shame and fear, but Joe shook his head. "I could see him plain as day, Dwight, but don't worry, I won't say anything. Maybe he was after those wolves. Man, what a dog!"

If there could be a better friend anywhere in the world than Joe Turnbull, Dwight didn't know who he could be. Maybe baseball had taught Joe fair play. Dwight felt that his friend saw now that the dog wasn't getting a fair deal. He felt better. Joe had courage; he might prove to be a good friend to the dog, in time of need.

CHAPTER NINE

THE SAME WOLF HOWL THAT AWAKENED BUCKY the morning of the wolf drag also awakened the big dog. He had spent the last few nights in a strawstack. His great strength had made it possible for him to dig deeply into the stack. Ventilation was poor, but he was still making the best of things. Safety counted more than comfort, and the den from which he had driven the coyotes was no longer safe.

He was now a lean, tough, hardy forager that was well able to take care of himself anywhere. Only one thing frightened him badly—a gun.

That savage howl came faintly to the big mutt, but he knew the wolves were close or he would not have heard it at all. He came raging out of the strawstack when he heard the howl, and stood there listening, his heavy head moving from side to side as he tried the icy wind.

The he-wolf did not howl again. He went slinking after his mate, who was bolder only because she was hungrier. Death lives always at the side of the wild thing, and when it braves danger, it is usually only because of fear of a greater danger.

In the she-wolf's case, the greater danger was starvation. Her mate could have waited longer. She could not.

The big mutt caught their scent faintly and went loping across the snow, growling threats. Soon there was no scent in the air to lead him, as the wolves moved on, but in a few minutes he picked up their trail on the bare, red, wind-swept slope north of the ranch. He followed it silently, knowing that any noise might bring out men—and guns.

The wolves had circled widely, coming almost in sight of Bucky Turnbull's place before turning back toward the Jeromes'. Bucky had no dogs; they would have caught the wolf scent and raised an alarm. While Bucky was telephoning the sheriff, the wolves were crossing his own range, heading for the Jerome ranch.

The wind brought them the sheep scent strongly. It also brought them the scent of Patch, while it blew their own telltale scent in the other direction. Patch slept on. With the she-wolf leading still, the two gaunt killers crept closer and closer.

Then two things happened—the wind suddenly brought them the scent of the outlaw mutt on their trail, and Mr. Jerome came to the door and put Colleen outside. His voice came clearly: "Out you go! You can sleep in the coalpit. It's about time you started to earn your keep, old girl."

The words meant nothing to the wolves, but observation had taught them that the night was for their own kind, and that man was rarely awake at this hour. Something was wrong! Instinct made them flinch back, hunger or no hunger. The uneasy old he-wolf turned tail and ran, and this time his mate followed without protest.

Suddenly something barred their way, reeking of man scent and danger. It was the highway. The wolves had crossed many roads on their flight down from the North, but they had all been covered with snow. Here the snowplow had laid the oiled gravel bare, and men and horses and dogs and livestock had used it often. Here the old he-wolf stopped.

A pair of lights rushed toward them, and they heard for the first time the close roar of an automobile engine. It was a group of sheepmen on their way to the drag. The wolves darted into a brush-filled draw that seemed to offer protection. Here they cowered, pinned down by the growing stream of traffic as more cars carried more men for the drag.

The wolves did not know about the wolf drag, and the alarm clocks that were set, the guns that were oiled and waiting all over the county. But they knew something was wrong when the silent night became noisy.

The night vanished as they cowered. The voices of men rang out in all directions, and their last chance of escape was gone.

But the path back to the Badlands and safety had been open to them almost until daylight, had they only known it.

For the big mutt had left their trail. While the two wolves hid in the brush, the dog was frisking gaily about the Jerome yard with Colleen. He made no tracks. The snow had long since been packed hard by feet and wheels and hoofs. A good thing too, for he had forgotten all about men and guns and danger.

Most dogs mate in the late spring. Nature has seen to this, since only those whose puppies had a summer growing time could survive the long, cruel centuries of wildness.

But Colleen was not altogether a product of nature. She was a show dog, and her father and mother had been show dogs, and all their fathers and mothers before them, for generations. Puppies born too early in the spring were saved by heated kennels and balanced diets. Even the weaklings that would have been weeded out under the harsh terms of natural law managed to survive.

In these weaklings, the fierce hunting instinct had also weakened. It had taken the hated wolves to revive it in Colleen. The mother instinct was not so strong, either. Colleen, the offspring of too many of these weaklings, was three years old and had never had puppies.

But the mother instinct was still there. When Mr. Jerome let her out of the house, the tall hound prowled the yard uneasily. The wolves were down-wind from her, but the big mutt was loping down out of the Badlands on their trail. She caught his scent and ran to join him. They met, and he forgot all about the wolves and let her coax him into the yard.

Colleen ran for the coalpit. The big mutt followed her as far as the door, where he stood whining. From the house came the smell of frying ham and eggs, an odor he remembered well and with longing. A light suddenly glowed in the attic, and he heard the voices of the boys as they wrestled on the bed. Once he had eaten such food, joined in such rough fun. He stood there at the coalpit door, whining and wagging his tail.

Patch, the new collie, had also heard the wolf howl. He had barked his reassuring answer to Mr. Jerome's call. He heard the big mutt come into the yard, but this did not upset him as a wolf or coyote would have done. He heard Colleen come bounding out of the coalpit. The two huge dogs raced back and forth through the dark, playing like overgrown puppies.

A door opened, and the sound of voices, the click of a bolt on a well-oiled rifle, warned the big mutt. He forgot all about Colleen as he tucked his tail between his legs and ran.

Immediately he crossed the trail of the wolves, and once more his brute mind took up where it had left off. He trailed them to the pavement, and then into the draw. They retreated from him, snarling. And suddenly, the dog heard men all around him. He smelled their guns. He heard them coming closer and closer, as the lines drew together. As he had hidden from men in New York alleys, so did he creep deeper and deeper into the brush now, while the wolves could only slink back and forth, whimpering.

He almost ran when Dwight shot the she-wolf, and the report of the rifle came cracking and echoing up the draw. He half jumped up, and then the old he-wolf came gliding down through the brush, and they met face to face.

The dog could not help himself then. His hatred of the wolf was more deeply ingrained than his fear of men, since it had been born in him, and his knowledge of guns was only a few weeks old. The wolf was cornered. It must fight at last. He crouched and gathered his feet under him, ready to close with it.

Then Dwight came into sight, and the rifle cracked, and the wolf screamed with agony. The dog stood up, trembling all over. Bill Ehmken fired from the bank, and the wolf lay still.

It was that second rifle that kept the dog from bolting out into the open. As he hesitated, quivering with terror, he heard one sharp, familiar word.

"Down!"

The dog lay down, as he had been taught to do at this word. The boy walked over and dragged the dead wolf up the bank. The big mutt lay there obediently, his nose wrinkling at the mixture of boy scent and wolf scent and gun scent—at the confusing blending of friendliness and danger.

The hunt moved on. The guns roared again and

again. The dog could stand it no longer. He turned and went crashing up the ditch to where it disappeared just below the bare slope. He came out into the open, running hard, heading for the Badlands.

But by then he was out of sight of the wolf drag, which had crossed the highway and was moving down toward his old den where the coyotes, who had reclaimed it, would be killed. In a little while he slowed down. He tucked his tail between his legs and trotted in aimless circles.

He was hungry again. Hunger sent him hunting, and while the hunters who had tried to kill him were eating lunch at the roadside, he came into Vaughn Jacobs' shed in broad daylight. He made his kill, leaped the back fence, circled through Bucky Turnbull's north range, and headed once more for the Badlands.

In a little while he heard Colleen following him. He sat down and waited for her. The hound came up, frisking. When he followed, she turned back toward the ranch, trying to lure him down there again.

The big mutt had been too thoroughly scared today for that. He followed her only a little way. Then he turned and headed once more into the Badlands.

Colleen followed him, timidly at first. In a little while she had caught up with him and ran almost at his side. When they started after a jack rabbit and broke into their wild, deep, musical baying, they were too far from any house to be heard.

Between them they wore the rabbit down, just as a pair of wolves as big and strong as they would have worn it down. They carried it to shelter under an overhanging bank. Here the big mutt slept, tired and lazy and gorged with mutton, miles from any sign of man, while his mate picked the rabbit clean.

Colleen missed her warm fireside that night, but when she grew cold she crept up beside the big mutt, and the two huge dogs warmed each other in the way of wild things.

Sheriff Lang and Deputy Bill got back to the courthouse early that afternoon. While the sheriff cleaned their guns, Bill studied the big map on the wall. On it he had marked every place where the big dog had been reported. Its "sure" killings were marked in red. Its old den, and all other places where tracks had been positively identified, were in blue. There had been dozens of other reports, of people "seeing" the big mutt. Most of these were doubtful, and these Bill had marked in orange.

"He sure gets around," the sheriff said.

Bill frowned. "He can't be two places at once, Cecil, and according to this map, he has been. I've been thinking. Maybe we're going at this thing all wrong. Maybe Dwight's right about him."

"Meaning—?"

"That maybe the wolves did some of the killings that are blamed on him."

The sheriff chuckled. "Bucky got a look at a couple of dead wolves today. Now maybe he'll believe there are such things."

Bill paced the room restlessly, glancing again and again at the map. "Maybe if we let Dwight try to catch him with a little kindness . . ."

The ringing of the telephone interrupted. The sheriff answered it.

"Hello, Sheriff Lang speaking. . . . Oh, yes, Vaughn, what can I do for you?" He listened a moment, his face growing gloomier. "All right, we'll be right out."

"Now what?" said Bill.

"Kindness, eh?" said the sheriff. "Tell Vaughn Jacobs that. He's got another dead sheep, and this time there's no mistake about what killed it."

"The dog?"

"The dog!"

By the time they got to the Jacobs place, nearly fifty sheepmen had gathered there in the shed, drawn by the news that though two wolves had been killed, their hard day's hunting had failed, after all. The dog's tracks were plain in the deep snow. Vaughn Jacobs, ordinarily a quiet, friendly man, was bitterly angry.

"You let a stray dog make fools of us!" he shouted.

"I did the best I could," said the sheriff. "If anyone has a better idea, I'm ready to listen."

Bucky Turnbull shook his fist. "I told you that wolf drag was a fool idea. It's about time we took the law into our own hands."

"Go ahead, and see where it gets you," came a quiet voice. Clayton Jerome came pushing through the crowd. He faced the angry men. "It's a free country, and I guess talk is the freest thing in it. Vaughn, I warned you not to build your sheepshed so far from the house. Well, you went ahead and did it anyway, and then I told you to get five or six good dogs, to play safe. But you didn't want to feed that many, and now you're paying for it. What do you expect Bill and Cecil to do—sit up all night with your sheep?"

"It's all right for you to talk," snapped Vaughn. "He didn't get any of your sheep."

"No, but the wolves did, and today we got some wolves. A good day's work, I call it. We've been lucky around here for a long time. Well, our luck caught up with us. We've had the worst winter in history and it's not over yet. The country just can't support all of us—our families, the sheep, the coyotes, the wolves, and now this wild dog. There just isn't enough food and shelter to go around, and something has to die."

"You and your balance of nature!" Bucky grumbled.

Mr. Jerome nodded. "Well, I won't harp on it. Sure, the dog is a bad actor! We've got to get rid of him, but you can't do it with hotheaded talk. I've noticed people always want to take the law into their own hands, just when they need it worst. Bill and Cecil are both good men. We knew it when we elected Cecil, and when he appointed Bill. They haven't changed, have they? Are they supposed to be peace officers or dog catchers? This is a new problem, and we've got to meet it in a new way."

"What new way?" Bucky asked angrily.

"I don't know. I'm a sheepman, so I never give advice to hunters or policemen. That way, I don't look silly as often as those who do. Ask Cecil or Bill."

"I haven't got the answer yet," Bill said soberly. "I'll see what I can figure out, since I'm supposed to be the hunter. Meanwhile, you'd all better keep a night watch over your sheep. You're going to lose more of them if you don't. I'm sorry, but that's the best I can do now."

"That's good enough for me," said Mr. Jerome. "Let's go home and get ready, Dwight. Tonight we stand guard."

Dwight had been listening in guilty silence. He and Joe had let the dog get away scot free. They were to blame for this dead sheep.

"We're a fine pair of sheepmen," Joe murmured.

"Maybe we ought to say something," Dwight whispered.

But he was glad when Joe whispered back, "Don't you dare!"

CHAPTER TEN

IT IS IMPOSSIBLE FOR WILD THINGS to break the moral laws of God and man, because no one has ever told them that such laws exist. The laws they break are natural ones, and their transgressions are acts of foolishness, rather than of evil. The wild thing that drops off to sleep without first seeing to his safety, and to a means of escape if that safety is disturbed, has broken the first of all natural laws, that of self-preservation. His punishment, as a rule, is quick and sure.

If the wild way—kill or be killed—looks savage to man, it is because the wild things must take the world as they find it, enemies and all. They can change nothing.

Man, on the other hand, is king of creation. He gets more out of the world than any of the wild creatures—more of food, more of warmth, more of comfort, more of peace, unless he himself breaks that peace. It is not much to man's credit that the way the wild things live with each other often turns out to be much less savage than the way man lives with men.

The big outlaw mutt had certain advantages over both the wild things and mankind, since he had born in him all the wild instincts, while at the same time he had lived with man long enough to know his ways. He knew so much about man, in fact, that he had almost a knowledge of right and wrong.

He was wild now, living under the hard, live-or-die rule of the wild things. But not long back he had been tame, living under a soft, simple, do-or-don't rule. When he was naughty he was punished—at least sometimes. When he was good he was rewarded—at least sometimes.

Those old rules had not been easy to learn, either. He must not dig in flower beds, or upset garbage cans, or run after cars, or go into meat markets, or growl at people on the street. On the other hand, if he snarled at a stranger in a dark hallway at night, and that stranger ran away and never came back, people praised him and scratched his odd little lop ears. No, they were not simple, these rules of the city, but he had learned them.

With them, he had learned a little about good and evil—not much, but more than the coyotes and wolves would ever know. He did not have a conscience, as human beings have one, but he had something pretty close to it.

Long after Colleen wanted to go home, the outlaw mutt kept her in the Badlands, simply because he knew at last that he was an outlaw. Until now he had been guiltless—afraid, perhaps, but not aware that he had committed a crime. His first sheep had been killed because he was hungry and, like everything else alive, he knew he had a need to live. This was the wild law, which makes a need a right.

The guns had taught him that it was unsafe to kill openly. Yet he had gone on killing sheep because he was hungry . . . and because he knew he could get away with it. But something had happened to make this last killing worse than the others, to make him more fearful of being caught than ever before. It was a simple thing—one word spoken in a firm voice: *"Down!"*

The habit of obedience was strong in the big mutt, but there was more to it than that. For that one instant his simple, faithful brute mind had the master it needed, and had never had. There are such things as one-man dogs, and the mutt was one, only he had never met his man until he met him in a snow-filled, brushy ditch, with a wolf lying dead between them. The man and woman had fed and caressed him. They had made him obey, after a fashion, but they had never commanded his deep, loyal respect the way Dwight Jerome had commanded it with just one word.

The dog ran out of the ditch and legged it up the slope because he feared the guns—and because he had gotten up after Dwight ordered, "Down!" After he killed Vaughn Jacobs' sheep, he ran because he feared Dwight Jerome and the punishment he knew he deserved. Having once more obeyed a human being, he feared more than ever to disobey. And it was odd how his loneliness increased as his fear increased.

For a week he ranged the Badlands, with Colleen constantly trying to coax him down to the ranch.

Now suddenly she would no longer follow him. One day she turned without warning, and snapped at him. This he ignored, but when she turned southward he followed her for hours. Now he was the one to coax; now Colleen was the one to go her way, letting him follow or stay, as he chose.

In this week, uproar had followed uproar among the sheepmen, as a new series of bloody raids took place. The first victim was Arnold Hoffman, who lost five sheep just two nights after the wolf drag. The next night it was Tex Lee, with two—the next, Nils Haberstroh with two. Nils' brother, Otto, lost two *the same night*. And on the following night, while Otto stood guard in one sheepshed, something came into his other shed, killed a ewe, and dragged her off nearly a quarter of a mile. The quarreling of the coyotes just before daylight brought Otto to the spot.

No family was more respected than the Hoffmans. Arnold, the father, was a county commissioner, a tall, quiet old man who said little, but whose eyes crinkled easily with silent laughter. His six sons were all grown; the family owned thousands of acres of Badlands range, and thousands of sheep. Yet the three eldest Hoffman boys had gone off to war, leaving their father and three younger brothers to do double work.

Tex Lee had once worked for the Hoffmans as a hired man. This was only his second year as an independent sheepman. Tex had a girl, a North Dakota girl. Sometimes he got lonesome for the sunny Rio Grande valley, in this cold, hard, lonely country. "Grapefruit as big as a pumpkin down there," he said. Texans wander far. But Tex was ready to give up and go back home that morning he found two dead sheep.

"Don't, Son," said Arnold Hoffman. "My boys and I will see you through. Sheepmen stick together."

The Haberstrohs were from Schleswig-Holstein, where Germany and Denmark come together. Their name was German, their accent Danish. They too had worked for the Hoffmans, until they could save enough money for a ranch of their own. Later there were two ranches, one for Nils and one for Otto. They were proud of their success, proud of the families they had raised here. "It's a hard country," they said, "but it's a poor man's country. Sure, our boys have to walk to school five miles! But at least there's a school."

Nils was short and fair, and full of laughter. Otto was the young one, the tall one, the one quick to anger. To have a sheep stolen under his very nose made him furious.

Deputy Bill came out and searched for tracks, but the hard-crusted snow kept the secret.

"Wolves, probably, by the way it was done," Bill said. "Were you keeping a night watch?"

Tempers were high. Otto flared: "I can't be two places at once, and I don't want those sheep mixed up. Two nights in a row. I can't stand much of this."

"It's better to mix them up than lose them," Bill advised. "I wish you people would realize that these old Saskatchewan cruisers are big-animal killers, not mouse hunters like the coyotes. Jacobs hasn't lost any, since he started keeping night watch. Neither has Bucky. Neither has Clay Jerome."

"But Clay's hound was stolen, wasn't she?" said Otto furiously. "I suppose the wolves did that. Don't talk to me about wolves! Nothing but a sheep-killing dog is smart enough to raid the same place two nights in a row."

"Wolves are, Otto," said Bill patiently, "and if you don't get all your sheep together where you can watch them, they'll be back again."

He didn't blame Otto for being angry. There were many mouths to feed here, and Otto worked hard. He could ill afford to lose sheep.

Studying his map that evening at the courthouse, Bill shook his head again and again. No dog could get around to so many places in so short a time. It had to be wolves, at least two wolves, maybe more.

"Got to give the dog the benefit of the doubt this time," he said.

He was marking the latest outrages on his map, in orange, when Sheriff Lang came in.

"More snow tonight, the radio says," the sheriff remarked.

"Oh?" Bill said absently.

"Yes. By the way, Dwight Jerome's dog came back."

"Oh?" Then Bill seemed to hear the sheriff for the first time. "Colleen came back?" he asked sharply.

"Yes. Pretty thin, Clay says. Why?"

"Don't you see, Cecil—the outlaw won't be far away from her," Bill cried. "With fresh snow coming, we'll have a chance to track him. An idea has been knocking at the door of my mind for a long time. I think I'll let it in. Boss, what would we do if it were a human being, a city gangster, hiding out in the range?"

"Why, swear in a posse and go after him, I suppose," the sheriff said thoughtfully.

"That's right! We've had this rascal on the run a couple of times. Let me have five or six good men who can shoot and ride, and who can be spared from home to stay as long as necessary, right on his trail. Let them be sworn in so they can draw a little pay, and so we'll have the legal right to go anywhere, and let me get on that dog's trail tomorrow morning in fresh snow. Then let me camp on it until I get him."

The sheriff thought it over. "County commissioners meet tomorrow. They'd have to authorize it, and I hate to ask them to appropriate extra money."

"Give me this chance. If I can't bring him in this time, I'll turn in my badge."

"Let me sleep on it," said the old sheriff firmly.

The dog followed Colleen almost home. It was not quite dark when they came in sight of the ranch, but a light already glowed in one end of the sheepshed. This was the "dope room," where Mr. Jerome kept his medicines and his other sheepman's supplies. Here there were two bunks and a good stove, for here he and Dwight spent most of their time during the lambing season. Here, also, they had taken turns sleeping ever since the wolf drag.

Patch came rushing at Colleen as she slipped through the corral fence. She was a stranger to the collie now, with the wild scent strong on her. Colleen ignored him. She went straight to the dope room door and whined.

Dwight was working on his next day's lessons by lantern light. He recognized that whine. With a cry, he threw down his book and opened the door. He dropped on his knees, and the tall hound crept in on her belly and put her head in his lap, whining for forgiveness.

"Colleen, Colleen, you're a worse traitor than I am," he choked, hugging her. "I thought you were gone for good."

134

He heard Patch race across the corral, barking frantically. He got to the fence just in time to see the big mutt vanish into the darkness. He stood staring longingly as the big brute ran up the slope. For a long time he leaned against the corral fence, stirred to the depths of his soul by the strength and speed and grace of the dog.

Up at the coalpit, Irene and Christine were filling the coal buckets. They heard the hound barking and ran to the house, screaming, "Daddy, Daddy—Colleen's back!"

With all three girls running beside him, Mr. Jerome came down to the sheepshed. The children flung themselves on the hound, and Colleen beat the floor with her tail and licked the hands that were stroking her so lovingly.

"She looks run to death," Mr. Jerome said. "Put her on a chain and keep her in the dope room. She's not going to get many more chances. Was the outlaw with her when she showed up?"

"Well . . . he was hanging around."

"Why didn't you take a shot at him?"

The loaded Arisaka leaned against the wall, in easy reach. Dwight looked down at the floor.

"I—I don't know, Dad. I just forgot."

"Next time, remember. Let's see if I can speed him on his way a little, anyway."

Mr. Jerome walked out to the fence with the gun. It was too dark to see anything, but he fired three shots up the slope anyway.

From the darkness came a frightened yelp, and

then silence. Mr. Jerome returned to the dope room and put the gun away, not noticing how white and tense Dwight had become, and how slowly the color came back to his face when he knew the dog had gotten away safely.

The dog heard the twang of those copper-jacketed bullets. He tucked his tail between his legs and ran, and not until he was again deep in the Badlands did he stop. Without Colleen he was lonely. He felt more lost than ever.

The wind had shifted slightly to the east. It was somewhat warmer. There would be snow tonight, and he needed shelter. But first he needed something to eat. He had been living on jack rabbit for a week, and the greedy Colleen had taken most of this lean fare. Now, without her help, it would be next to impossible to catch them. Winter had made the jacks lean and fast, and only the toughest and fastest were still alive.

He sat down and howled, but Colleen did not come—did not even answer. The thick flakes began to fall, slowly at first, then heavier and heavier. A week's wildness had somewhat dulled his memory of Dwight's voice. When he realized at last that Colleen was not coming back, he turned and headed toward Bucky Turnbull's place, running strongly, driven by hunger.

Coming in sight of the sheepshed, the dog stopped. A lantern hung in each end of it. He hesitated a long time, until he heard Bucky's alarm clock ring inside the house. Bucky came out with his rifle under his arm, to make sure his sheep were safe. He had no warm dope room, but he was rising every hour at night until the danger was over. The dog faded back without ever showing himself.

At Vaughn Jacobs' shed there was a comfortable bunk room, with a light in it. There were three dogs here now—not all good sheep dogs, because good sheep dogs had become scarce, and in demand. But they could scent a strange dog, and when they barked Walt Trescoli ran out of the bunk room with a powerful flashlight in one hand and his rifle in the other. He saw the dog lurking in the grove. He dropped the flashlight to take one wild shot, as the dog slipped away between the trees.

Again the dog heard the scream of a bullet, the flat crack of a gun. Then the light whisper of the snow was the only sound anywhere. Still he ran until Vaughn Jacobs' place was miles behind.

He came to the schoolhouse and nosed about the yard, but there was no food here, and no shelter. He ran on.

Everywhere he prowled, it was the same story. Men were now guarding their sheep as they guarded their lives, with lights and guns and vigilance. For sheep *were* life in this country where nothing else useful grew. Aroused at last, the sheepmen were giving battle. This winter of high drifts, of night raids, of cold night watches, of lanterns and loaded guns and sleepless vigilance was one they would never forget.

Several times, the dog crossed the sign of skulking wolves, but these savage killers stayed out of his way. They were hunting in desperate pairs, two pairs of them, and it was not the big mutt they feared, but the other dogs and the armed men who might be attracted to a fight.

The two pairs of wolves were prowling from ranch to ranch. One by one, they too were finding lights and guns and men on guard.

The merciless fist of famine was being closed tighter and tighter. The snow covered everything. There were thousands of frozen carcasses of cattle and sheep all over the West, but the deep drifts covered them and not even the keen noses of the wolves would find them until the spring thaws came. Spring would be too late for these savage old Saskatchewan cruisers.

Now the wolves must watch and wait, with the patience that only hungry wild things have. Sooner or later some man would turn his back to go into the house for a cup of coffee or to warm himself. It took nerve to strike, to kill, to eat, to escape, all in the brief time a man's back was turned. And sheep dogs would fight, and life would be measured in the running steps of a raging sheepman.

Patience and nerve, and then speed and luck— these were the price of survival for the great northern wolves.

The dog came at last to the town itself, without

finding a single unguarded ranch. It was not late, but only a few lights showed. People were becoming accustomed to the storm, ready to "den up" like the wild things until it ended. The dog, being city-bred, had no fear of town. He trotted boldly down the streets. A dog challenged him here and there from under a warm porch, but his size awed them, and he ignored their barking.

In a little while he heard voices.

A man and a woman were walking along through the snow, arm in arm. Deputy Bill Ehmken and the schoolteacher had been to Sheriff Lang's house for supper. Deputy Bill wanted his boss and his future wife to know each other. This weekend Miss Stevenson was spending in town, with Bill's folks. As soon as he could spare the time, Bill was going to take a week off and visit the Stevensons in Minneapolis.

The dog followed them a short distance, drawn by human voices that were not raised in anger against him. The words meant nothing, but he felt the sympathy in the woman's voice.

"Poor Dwight!" she was saying. "It will break his heart when that dog is killed, and it will break mine to see him."

"I know," said Bill, "and the worst of it is, Laura, he's right! That dog could be a good dog, in good hands."

"Then why kill him?" she asked.

"Because he kills sheep, dear. This is a hard

country. When you take our sheep, we have nothing left."

"But must Dwight be part of your old posse, if there is a posse? He did his share when he killed the wolves. He's too young to be on a posse. I shudder to think of what might happen. Look at how he went down into that awful ditch after those wolves. Why does he have to help?"

"Because if he doesn't, we won't catch the dog, and that's the size of it," said Bill. "It's queer how much depends on a little shaver just fifteen years old. I'm a hunter, but I'm not hunter enough for this job. If we get that dog, this country will owe Dwight Jerome more than it can ever pay."

"It already does, because of those wolves!" Miss Stevenson burst out. "I still think it's unfair."

"I didn't say it was fair. I just said it had to be. Dwight's a sheepman's son. He'll be ready to go whenever Cecil says the word. And I wish he'd say it soon so we can get this over with."

She pressed his arm. "Poor dear, you're not enjoying this much either, are you?"

They went into the house, and the dog turned and followed their trail backward, lonesomely. It brought him finally to Sheriff Lang's little frame cottage at the edge of town.

The sheriff had been a sheepman until persuaded to run for office years ago. Even now, he kept a cow and chickens. A kindhearted man, he had a wide, shallow pan just outside his barn door. Each morning and evening he filled it with milk for the neighborhood cats. When his cow ran dry each spring, he bought canned milk for them. The cats, he said, were his Maltese sheep—"Maltese and Persian and tabby, and a little purebred this-and-that."

The sheriff had no deep knowledge of wild animals, but he had a wide, unsuspicious love of all tame ones. He felt guilty about being so late with his milking tonight, but first there had been extra work in the office, and then company for supper. He had to wait until Bill and Laura Stevenson were gone.

When he came out of the barn with his pail of milk, a dozen cats were complaining bitterly beside the pan.

"It's a good thing you can't vote," he said, as he poured out their warm milk. "I guess you don't think I'm a very good sheriff, do you? Well, neither does anyone else lately."

He gave them a little extra tonight. Then he went in and went to bed. He was soon asleep.

A few minutes later his wife shook him awake.

"Cecil, did you feed that pack of cats tonight?"

"Yes, why?" he asked sleepily.

"There must be a dog there, stealing their milk. Such a commotion I've never heard."

The sheriff sat up. "I don't hear anything."

"He must be gone now. Maybe it's that outlaw.

No ordinary dog could get over a six-foot fence."

"Neither could he. Now, go to sleep!"

Once again the sheriff was wrong.

It is a mistaken belief, held by many people, that dogs cannot climb. Wolves and foxes and coyotes do, quite expertly, perhaps not so nimbly as cats, nor in the same way. But their eternal search for food makes it necessary for them to do many things, and when they must climb to eat, they climb.

Likewise with dogs. Some hunting breeds, notably raccoon and foxhounds, will follow game right into a tree. The coon or cat goes to the highest branches. The dog climbs as high as he can, falls to the ground, climbs up again . . . and falls again and again and again. Many times he can get down only by falling; some dogs can climb up, but not down. Many a dog has been stranded high in a tree, to be brought down the next morning in some disgusted man's arms.

The big mutt had climbed that six-foot fence. His great Dane blood gave him strong forelegs, which he used almost like human arms. He had not tasted milk in a long time. The pan tempted him, and so did those spitting cats, whose New York relatives had furnished him with so much forbidden amusement.

The dog half jumped, half climbed up the woven wire netting. He fell over the top heavily and lighted squarely among the cats, sending them snarling and squalling into the dead weeds of the sheriff's garden patch. He lapped up the warm milk greedily, and still he was hungry.

The dog had never stolen chickens before. The sheriff's chicken house was tight and warm, but it was an old building, and the weathered wood had become spongy with age. The door was closed, but the dog did not want to make a noise on this side, next to the house, anyway.

Behind the house he found a board that was curled and warped. He got his powerful teeth on the protruding edge, and pulled. Part of it splintered off, and he then could get one of his strong forelegs into the crack. The rest was easy.

Inside the house, the fat old hens slept soundly on the roosts, their heads under their wings. Somehow the dog knew they could raise more racket than sheep, but somehow he knew what to do too.

He put his big nose gently between two of them. His warm breath made them feel good. Slowly pushing, he thrust one away from the other, making her pinch her way along the roost. Still her head remained under her wing, and she snuggled against his head as trustingly as she had been snuggling against the other hen.

He nudged her sharply with his nose. She took her head out from under her wing—and the dog grabbed it. There was a brief flapping racket that disturbed the other hens slightly. He ate.

He killed a second hen the same way. This one,

he took back over the fence with him for Colleen.

But the wolfhound had been fed well tonight, and now slept on a chain beside Dwight's cot in the dope room. The big mutt could not tempt her with his stolen chicken. He left the feathers of the sheriff's hen scattered over the snow less than a quarter of a mile north of the Jerome corral.

Bill Ehmken got the sheriff's call early in the morning.

"My mind is made up, Bill. Start calling your people. Let's have a posse in the saddle by noon. I'll take a chance on the commissioners."

"Fine, but what changed your mind?" Bill asked.

"I'll tell you later. This is a party line."

A fine thing, the sheriff thought, when a dog came into town and stole his chickens right out from under his nose! The old man had troubles enough without advertising this new indignity all over the county on a party line. He could understand people's terror better now. A dog that big, that bold, that smart—well, he didn't blame them for wanting him hunted down.

CHAPTER ELEVEN

"HOLD UP YOUR RIGHT HANDS."

Dwight looked past the sheriff and out of the window at the silently falling snow. His hand came up slowly. His heart rebelled at this oath. He thought bitterly: *It's supposed to be an honor, but not for me! Why do I have to do it—why, why, why?*

The answer, of course, was that he was a sheepman's son. Many an older man has been just as bitter and rebellious on learning, for the first time, what heavy burdens honors can be.

His mother and the girls watched from the kitchen door. From behind them came the tantalizing odors of chicken and noodles, fresh bread about ready to come from the oven, and custard pies sprinkled with nutmeg. A hot meal, Mrs. Jerome said, was the right start for a cold ride. A hot meal was her solution for many things.

The sheriff cleared his throat. "Now, repeat after me, 'I do solemnly swear to uphold and defend . . .' "

"I do solemnly swear to uphold and defend," Dwight murmured.

Beside him Bucky Turnbull was gruff and impatient with all this falderal. On Dwight's other side Walt Trescoli sounded grave and a little fearful. So did Emil Hoffman, old Arnold's tall, quiet son. Emil was thirty. Like Bill Ehmken, he was a veteran of the Pacific wars, while Walt had served in Europe. The oath stirred memories for these two.

Beyond Emil, Joe Turnbull repeated the words loudly. Joe had his own reasons for being here. His name had not been on Bill's list. He had arrived at the last minute, just this morning.

"I'm going with you, so you might as well swear me in," he said, "because I'm going whether you do or not."

"Oh, no!" his uncle cried. "You get back home, boy, or I'll tan your britches for you good!"

Joe had grown a lot this last year, and Bucky was a small man. Perhaps he had not realized how much his lanky nephew towered over him.

Joe smiled. "You'd better cut a pretty long stick, Uncle Bucky, because I'm going."

Bucky appealed angrily to the sheriff. "Leave these kids at home. They'll just help that dog get away! I don't think it's legal to deputize kids anyway. This is a man's job!"

"How about that, Bill?" the sheriff asked.

"We need Dwight," said Bill. "Either we've got an emergency or we haven't. If we have, we can deputize anyone who can make himself useful.

If we haven't, then what's all this fuss about? Let them go."

After the oath, Joe got a chance to whisper to Dwight: "They're not so smart! Anything you think of to do, you count on me. They're not going to kill that dog."

Dwight's father was watching them. He knew boys just about as well as he knew animals. Dwight fingered the special deputy's badge, which seemed so heavy on his shirt.

"No, we can't do anything, Joe," he said. "But we can make sure he doesn't suffer."

A quick, merciful death . . . surely they wouldn't begrudge the outlaw that. But as he watched the grim faces of Walt and Emil and Bucky, as they ate, he was not so sure. These men hated the dog bitterly.

The posse went out to where Mr. Jerome had their saddled horses. They mounted and turned their backs to the snow for the sheriff's last instructions.

This was not like the terrible blizzard of a few weeks ago. There was no wind. The big flakes sifted down quietly. But Dwight knew this peacefulness was a lie. Nature itself had turned against the dog. Wherever in flight it set foot in this clean, white snow, its tracks would betray it.

"You're officers of the law now," the sheriff said. "You'll do your duty and follow orders and live up to your oaths, and if any one of you has been wondering why the law didn't do something—

well, here's your chance. It's up to you now. I'll carry your camp gear in my car and I'll try to bring at least two hot meals a day from town. But it's the dog who'll decide where you spend your nights, not I. Good luck."

Mr. Jerome fussed with Limpy's cinches. In a low voice he said: "It's no fun, Dwight, but all your life you'll have jobs that aren't fun. Do the best you can. A lot of people are counting on you."

The posse followed Bill Ehmken out of the yard. The snow fell steadily as they trotted into the Badlands. While the ranch was yet in sight, Bill gave them his plan.

"I think he'll be hanging around here, close to Colleen. When we hit the slope, spread out. Keep in sight of each other. Two quick shots will be the signal that you've seen him. Don't be afraid to shoot the minute he shows up. You're not going to sneak up on him anyway. Keep track of which way he goes, so we can pick up his sign."

"Let's go," Bucky grumbled impatiently. He had moved his small flock over to Vaughn Jacobs' place. He was anxious to get this job done and go home and bring his sheep home.

They could hear Colleen's lonely howl for miles, until the Jerome place was no longer in sight. There was little talk. They reached the slope, and Bill sent Emil far to his right, with Bucky behind him. Walt and Joe he sent to the west.

"I want Dwight close to me," he said. "When we pick up the trail, I'll need him to read sign."

Almost at once two quick shots rang out from Emil Hoffman's gun. Dwight spurred over and found Emil and Bucky, looking down at fresh tracks in the snow. Bill came riding up as Dwight studied them.

"Well, Dwight?"

Dwight carefully brushed the fresh snow from the big paw prints. "Wolves, I think. Two of them, walking in each other's tracks."

"You've got wolves on the brain," Bucky muttered.

Bill paid no attention to him. "How old?"

Dwight squatted there, studying the tracks. Something was all wrong. They just didn't belong here, in broad daylight.

"About an hour, maybe," he said. "They're scared, or they wouldn't be here. Let's backtrack and find out why."

"Backtrack?" Bucky snorted. "If it is wolves, why don't we go after them?"

Walt and Joe rode up. Bill turned his horse and said: "I'm still giving the orders. Go ahead, Dwight."

Dwight, riding in the lead, heard Bucky muttering to Walt and Emil. Then Joe said something Bucky didn't like. This quarreling wasn't a good start.

The wolves had been running hard here, the smaller, lighter female following the male. She had run in his tracks, not to hide her own, but to save her strength by letting him break a trail through the deepening snow.

In a little while the single trail became two, as they came to the place where the female had dropped in behind her mate. Deputy Bill turned in the saddle, grinning broadly.

"Now what do you think, Bucky? Here's where they got good and scared and took off in a beeline, the way Dwight said. There's a scared, hungry pair of cruisers for you. I bet they're frisking around down at your place right now."

Bucky stared at the two trails, shaking his head. "Nobody could really tell that, though, from just looking at the one track," he said.

"Dwight can," Bill chuckled.

They rode on. In a few minutes the two sets of tracks veered aside to where there was a little mound of snow.

"Poisoned horse meat," Bill explained. "I've put out four hundred pounds, but none of it has been touched. Here's where they were nosing around when something scared them, isn't it?"

"Yes." Dwight's heart suddenly stood still. He wheeled Limpy over to the innocent-looking but deadly lump in the snow.

Not just the wolves, but the big mutt too had been here. And the poisoned meat *had* been disturbed. Dwight tumbled out of the saddle and knelt down. He had seen animals die of poison. Poison too was necessary as the sheepmen fought for survival in this lean, hard country. But again he remembered that fight between the mutt and the two wolves. Again his heart protested that the dog deserved a better death.

He studied the tracks, first in terror and then in thankfulness. The wolves were no smarter than the dog. He had turned the meat over and over, sniffing and snuffing and puzzling over it. But he had left it untouched.

"How long ago?" Bill asked.

"Not very long," said Dwight with a heavy heart.

He got back into the saddle. The dog had gone straight west from here, running hard. To judge by the snow that had fallen since, these tracks were made not more than fifteen or twenty minutes ago. About that time Emil Hoffman had fired those two shots on seeing the wolf tracks. Nothing but gunfire could have scared the dog this badly.

The posse broke into canter, and for once Bucky was not complaining. For over an hour they rode in silence, following a trail which continued to run straight as a string to the west. The dog had been going at a swift, strong lope that he could keep up for a long time. It was as though he knew that he was on the run, that this was a showdown, and was using his great strength to postpone death as long as possible.

And maybe he does know, Dwight thought with pity. Did animals sense the approach of death? Sometimes Dwight scoffed at the idea, but sometimes he wasn't so sure. He had watched wild things die. A kind of peace came over them, and they looked up at man with fear no longer in their eyes. To Dwight it seemed that they were going their wild way through some unmapped shadowland that was close to him and to all hunters, a sanctuary where nothing was hunted, and where there was a safe hiding place for everything.

What about the dog—would there be a hiding place for him? Would he know about that shadowland and the way to it, or would the tameness of having been owned by a human bar him? Would there be peace in his eyes as he looked up at them before he died?

Not all of the boy was in the squeaking saddle, listening to the panting of the horses, the steady thud of hoofs. A part of him was up there ahead with the dog, listening to the deep, deep silence of that shadowland, and running, running, running. . . .

The Jerome range had been left behind. These were strange slopes, strange hills. Somewhere to the south, the road turned and ran south to a junction with the Federal highway. Just a few miles beyond that corner was the little town where a man and a woman had found shelter from a storm—a weak city man and woman in the worst of all storms. Here they had assured each other, "Yes, it was the kindest thing, after all."

Now there were only winding local roads south of the posse, mere trails that turned and twisted through the wild, desolate Badlands into Montana. Dwight knew the dog had seen them and knew they were on his trail. The big mutt was on the run. He was being driven, and he knew it, and he was scared.

Dwight tried not to think about it. He sat up and looked around. Bucky Turnbull too was looking around, frowning. Dwight smiled to himself. Sheriff Lang might have trouble finding them tonight. No one had expected the dog to "line out" and lead them this far today. Well, let Bucky see what it was like to be caught out in a storm without food or shelter.

The others looked worried too. Of the six, only Dwight and Bill felt at home. They were the ones with the wild streak that forgot mealtime and bedtime. Well, let the others learn that too. It was not a simple thing to be a sheepman or a sheepman's son.

Dwight's heavy heart jumped suddenly, and he forgot his confused sadness in a great, unexpected thrill.

There, in plain sight less than a quarter of a mile ahead of them, was the big mutt!

He had stopped to nose along through the snow, investigating something or other. A jack rabbit had suddenly leaped out of a little wigwam of snow-covered grass and went sailing toward the horizon. A second later came the dog's deep hunting voice, belling back to them.

Bill Ehmken, startled, reined in.

"Look at him go!"

The dog heard. The baying stopped. Down came his tail. He left the rabbit's trail and went loping out of sight to the west.

When Bill Ehmken looked at Dwight, his face was white and sick.

"I see what you mean, Son," he said. "What a dog!"

"What are we waiting for?" Bucky shouted. "Let's go!"

"Just a minute," said Bill. "You're not going to catch him. Save your horses and let him run his head off. We've just started."

"But it's almost dark!" Bucky said angrily.

"That's right. You're not going home tonight, Bucky, and you might as well get used to the idea. If I remember rightly, there's an old sheepshed a few miles ahead of us, along the road. We'll bunk there tonight. Joe, go back down to the highway and wait for Cecil, and tell him where we are. Just keep straight west on the road, and you can't miss us."

"All right," Joe said doubtfully. He turned his horse, but several times he looked back over his shoulder. Soon he disappeared from view.

The others kept up a steady canter after the dog. In a little while they got another glimpse of him. He was just going over the crest of a slope and was quickly lost to view, but Dwight and Bill both saw that he had settled down to that easy, long-legged lope.

"He's not going to be easy to wear out," Bill said.

They saw him several times before dark fell, but without gaining on him. The footing here was easy for the dog, hard and dangerous for the horses. Emil and Bucky each had a bad spill.

He can't even take time to hunt, Dwight thought, with pity. *All he can do is run and run and run. . . .*

Only a little daylight remained when the posse came to the old sheepshed. The dog was somewhere out of sight, but not far ahead. Dwight was the last to leave the trail. He sat looking at those tracks in the dusk for a long time.

"You're worrying more about that dog than you are about us," Bucky accused him when he at last rode down to the shed.

Dwight did not answer.

One end of the old shed had fallen in, and its roof lay almost on the ground, but at the other end there was shelter for their horses and themselves. When Joe and the sheriff had not appeared by dark they pulled off a few old weathered boards and built a fire under the ramshackle eaves. They unsaddled, tied their tired, hungry horses under the shed, and sat around the fire in glum silence.

It was not a cold night, and the yapping of the coyotes, which came with increasing frequency, was like music to Dwight. Except for his pity for the dog, he might have enjoyed this night out in the open. He studied Bill, who had done his hard duty once before, but who was having no fun here, either. Did Bill really see how unfair all this was? Bill was a sheepman's son too. Did Bill realize that they were just taking it out on the dog for all of the hard luck and heartbreak the storm had brought? Whatever his thoughts, he was keeping them to himself.

It was hours before they heard the sheriff's car. They went down to the road to meet it and lead the way back between the drifts and rough spots. Joe was trotting his horse ahead of the car, and in the bright headlights he looked cold and tired and dejected.

"The next time you want someone to stand around all night in the snow, Bill, pick someone else!" he said angrily. "I thought I was lost, and I nearly froze to death before he got there."

"You wanted to be a deputy, didn't you?" Bill said, and his voice was a little sharper than usual. "Go sit by the fire and get warm. I told you this was no picnic."

"I didn't think you'd get this far," the sheriff said. "Everything is probably cold, but it's healthier that way. Yes, this will do you all good."

No one answered; the sheriff was having his little joke at their expense, after having been the target of their complaints for so long. He had three big cream cans, one holding macaroni soup, one boiled beef and rice, and one coffee. It was all barely lukewarm. They set the coffee can in the fire and ate ravenously, without waiting to warm the soup and beef.

Sheriff Lang had also brought barley and hay for the horses. He carried bedrolls in as they ate.

"I think of everything, you see. I take good care of my men," he joshed them solemnly. "Nice little camp you've got here. Always did love to sit around a campfire and hear horses stamping and pulling at their hay. It makes me wish I was twenty years younger."

"It looks foolish to me to stay out here all night," Emil Hoffman said. "Why can't we leave the horses here and come out and start in the morning?"

"That's a reasonable question," said Bill, "and I'll give you a reasonable answer. That dog's going to know if we leave. He'll know if we turn back too. We've got him on the run. Let's keep him on the run."

"That's right," said the sheriff. "Well, I'll see you about four thirty."

"Four thirty?" cried Walt. "It's almost midnight now."

The sheriff stopped with his hand on the handle of his car door. "That's about when the dog will wake up, Walt. Or do you want me to fix it up with him to wait until you get your sleep out? A while back you boys were all hollering for the law to hunt this dog down. Well . . . hunt him down!"

He got into the car and drove away. There was no more grumbling.

Long after the others were asleep, Dwight lay staring into the darkness. When he heard the dog howling, not far away, he had to fight hard to hold back the tears. He beat the ground with his fist.

"I won't, I won't, I won't!"

But he felt the badge on his shirt, and he remembered his oath and the years of heartbreak and hard work and self-denial that had made this a sheep country. In a little while it would be lambing time. This winter would be over, the dog forgotten, as another cycle of spring and sun and grass began. The sheep came first, or they were all lost, and all the work and heartbreak of the pioneers before them.

The fire had almost died down. Dwight fished in his shirt pocket for Bill's Distinguished Service Cross. He studied it by the red light that came from the coals. It had snowed on Okinawa too. There had been nights when Bill Ehmken slept as best he could, telling himself, "I won't, I won't, I won't!" Bill had talked quite a bit about Okinawa to Dwight. The boy knew something about soldiering.

At last he slept, with the badge, which he had unpinned, and the D.S.C. clutched in his fist.

CHAPTER TWELVE

THE SHERIFF'S NOISY OLD CAR AWAKENED THE posse promptly at four thirty; Cecil Lang was a man of his word. He fed their horses while they rebuilt the dead fire and squatted around it, munching the hot sausage and biscuits and hard-boiled eggs he had brought.

No one talked. Even Deputy Bill seemed morose and short-tempered.

It was snowing again before they finished eating. The fall had stopped during the night, but not for long. Unhappily they watched the sheriff roll up their warm sleeping bags and carry them out to the car. They saddled their squealing, fighting horses as the sheriff brought in their saddle rolls. These contained one blanket, a parcel of food, and a small bag of grain for each horse, all wrapped in a bed-size square of canvas. Tonight would be still more cheerless, if they had only these.

"It's hard to tell where you'll be, boys," the sheriff said in perfect good humor. "I'll try to get to you, but probably I won't be able to." He drove away, whistling.

The leaking old tumble-down shed looked too snug and pleasant a place to leave. They led their horses out with reluctance and mounted stiffly in darkness which, after the sheriff's car lights were out of sight, was darker than ever.

"His tracks will all be snowed in, but he'll make some more," Bill said. "I don't think he strayed far from here, do you, Dwight?"

"No," said Dwight. Somehow he knew the dog would keep them in sight all night. He had been somebody's dog once. He would hear their talk and smell their food, and—

"String out again, north and south, and wait for daylight," Bill was saying. "Two quick shots will mean you've spotted him again. I want Dwight here close to the road, with me. Let's go."

The horses bit at each other, possibly a sign of worse weather to come. Dwight and Joe picked their way together. The deep hush made the jingle of bits, the squeak of saddles, sound unnaturally loud. Joe was in a sullen, angry mood.

"I thought it over plenty last night," he said. "This dog's getting a bad deal. Dwight, are you going to let them get away with it?"

"What can we do?" Dwight stopped Limpy. He felt sick every time he thought of seeing the big dog kick his life out in the reddening snow, surrounded by vengeful men with smoking guns. "What can we do? It's a sheep country."

"Well, you better think of something," said Joe,

"because they're not going to kill that dog. Not Bill Ehmken or anybody else."

Dwight had never seen Joe so angry. All of his old happy-go-luckiness was gone. He had changed a lot in the last few days.

Joe's horse plodded on. In a few minutes, Bucky Turnbull rode past Dwight, and Dwight heard him grumbling at his nephew over who should ride on to the top of the slope. Joe refused to budge, so Bucky had to ride on.

Little by little the darkness lifted. Above Dwight was Joe, and beyond Joe was Bucky, hunched down in the saddle and shivering. Down by the road sat Bill, as still as an Indian in the saddle. Across the road was Walt, and far to the south, almost out of sight, was Emil.

They did not laugh or joke or call to each other. They merely waited. For an instant, Dwight could almost feel their hatred. For an instant the wild half of him trembled like a cornered animal. For an instant, *he* was the one being hunted—*he* was hiding from these men and their bitter, unfair hatred—*he* was running hopelessly from the guns.

The feeling passed, but something had come into Dwight's troubled soul that left him less of a boy, and more of a man. He knew now what he had to do.

Let the dog be killed by a friend, he thought. Not in hatred, but in mercy. Let him have this last hopeless victory over his enemies. Let him know, as he started down the trail into that unmapped shadowland where the wild things hide forever, that a friend had whispered, "Good luck and good hunting!"

Suddenly Dwight saw the dog.

He broke from cover, less than a hundred yards away, close to him and even closer to Bill Ehmken. Dwight's mouth came open with amazement as he stared.

For the dog too had spent the night in the old sheepshed. He had crawled in under the collapsed roof and had slept less than twenty feet from them, snug and dry and cozy.

Dwight quietly pulled the cold Arisaka from the saddle boot. The dog was sharply outlined against the white snow. He was poised tensely on three legs, his body twisted, ready to bolt in any direction. The massive head swung from side to side, as the dog sought to pick up the scent of his enemies.

Dwight centered his aim on the dog's spine, just ahead of the shoulders. His breaking heart said, *Good luck and good hunting!* His finger tightened on the trigger.

Then Joe Turnbull's horse smashed into Dwight's, and Joe's crazy face was less than a foot away, and Joe had hold of the rifle barrel. He was screaming, "No, no, you'd be sorry the rest of your life!" There were tears in Joe's eyes.

The dog bolted. Across the road, Walt Trescoli fired, and then Bill and Emil and Bucky all fired together. But the dog was already out of range.

Dwight knew his moment had passed. He slid the gun back into its boot. No matter what happened, he never could shoot the dog now. He turned his back to Joe, covered his face with his arm, and tried to hold back the sobs.

"How do you like that for nerve?" Bill shouted admiringly.

Bill could have shot the dog too. Dwight saw now that he just didn't want to. He'd go along and help hunt the dog down. He'd lead and command and give orders, but Bill's mind was also made up, whether he knew it or not. Someone else could pull the trigger.

They streamed after the dog, and Emil yelled: "If you two hadn't been roughhousing like a couple of ten-year-old kids, you might have shot him. Keep your mind on your work."

"I told you!" Bucky snorted. "I told you not to let kids go along. Every time you need them, they're playing."

Dwight and Joe looked at each other, and then away. The posse had misunderstood their brief scuffle. Joe would be in serious trouble if they knew the truth. Not that he cared, to judge by his sullen, downcast look.

"There he goes!" Walt cried. He snapped out his gun and fired a one-handed shot into the air.

The dog was running hard, not saving his strength. He had lain under the old roof all night, watching the men around their fire, yearning to creep up to them and take his scolding, and then be petted and fed and allowed to share their fire.

He was hungry. He had smelled their food this morning, but he knew no one would throw him a handful and say, "Here, this is for you." As strong as the food smell was the gun smell. So he lay and watched them, his simple brute heart torn between loneliness and fear.

From his hiding place, he had watched as the horses were led out. One by one, the riders disappeared into the snow and darkness. The dog raced up and down the old shed, greedily searching for scraps and crumbs, which were few.

There was no wind to bring him the scent of the posse. When at last he came out of shelter it was because he was hungry, and he thought they had gone away.

Joe's yell warned him almost too late. He streaked across the slope, not with the gliding grace of a wild thing but with the clumsy panic of a terrified city dog. Walt's bullet came close, filling him with still more terror. The dog tucked his tail between his legs and ran until his pounding heart and air-starved lungs demanded rest.

He sat down. In a little while the posse came in sight again, and the quick-eyed Walt fired. The dog turned and ran, and still his enemies came on.

He was suddenly no longer a completely wild thing. He was too scared and confused. The more he felt drawn back to mankind, the more his wild instincts failed him. He had been too long a city dog, a man's dog. Mankind too long had solved his problems for him. In his direst need he turned again to man, and man drove him away.

Several times that day he stopped when he could have run on. He did not hunt. He merely sat down in the snow, whining and looking back over his own trail, thumping the ground with his tail as he begged for forgiveness in his simple dog fashion. Each time, as the six riders came into sight again, he waited until it was almost too late. Each time he heard the twang of bullets, the bark of guns. Each time he ran on, with his tail between his legs.

This was what Bill Ehmken had meant when he said, "Keep him on the run." Bill knew the brute mind too, how panic could confuse it, and how confusion could waste the strength of a big brute body.

The dog's old, smooth, wolflike gait had saved his feet and legs. These lumbering, panicky leaps quickly made his legs swell and ache. The pads of his feet burned and became sore. By evening he was limping a little.

All this was quite clear in the trail he left, to anyone who could read it. It would hurt the heart of a silent, troubled boy who, reading it, rode on and on and on without hope.

For Dwight too was confused and frightened, caught in a cross fire of duty and justice. Dwight too had lost touch with nature. Like the dog, he felt betrayed and bewildered.

That night the posse found a small outcropping of lignite. The dog had circled to the northwest all afternoon, leading them farther and farther from any road. It had snowed most of the day, but at dusk it stopped. They built a lignite fire and ate their cold meal and gratefully crawled into their blankets.

The dog saw the fire and crept close to investigate. One of the tethered horses heard him and blew a warning flutter of breath. Bill Ehmken heard it in his sleep, and stirred.

Dwight was still awake. He raised himself on his elbow. He heard the dog whine not far away. He saw Bill move.

"No, no!" he said sharply.

The dog turned and ran. He heard a sleepy voice say, "What's the matter, Dwight?" Another voice answered, "Oh, something spooked the horses, I guess."

A mile away the dog stopped. Alone in the world, long ago abandoned by man and now betrayed by nature, he sat down and pointed his nose skyward. The coyotes became silent as they heard that deep, despairing howl. Dwight covered his ears and lay stiff and tense in his cold bed.

"What'll I do, what'll I do?" he asked Joe in the morning.

"I don't know," said Joe sullenly, "but you better think of something!"

The dog had swung north. He circled aimlessly at first, this third day. Not until the posse came close did he once more "line out." They pushed their horses to the limit, crowding him hard.

Once more the dog tucked his tail between his legs and fled, stopping to rest and whimper when he outdistanced them, again running clumsily with his tail between his legs when they came into sight and fired at him.

Always there were the guns. "Keep him on the run," Bill warned, again and again.

The posse kept him on the run.

The dog's pell-mell northward flight had led the posse into wilder, rougher country. Here the horses often found hard going. So did the dog, but by now hunger had become his greatest problem. He could not long keep up this pace without food, and there was little time to hunt. A jack rabbit jumped up in front of him. A few weeks ago, his hair-trigger wildness would have made him snap without thinking, and the rabbit would have been thrown into the air with a broken back.

But today it escaped, and he wore himself out following its nimble, zigzag trail. He was still running after it, hopelessly, when he heard the guns behind him again.

Night found him once more in livestock range, this time a rolling meadowland valley that wound and stretched and twisted between the hills. Here the posse found a little ranch, a house and corral and barn, with hay and grain and shelter for their horses, food and beds for themselves.

It had been a punishing day, with no rest, and

for food only the remnants in the little parcel the sheriff had brought. Even Dwight felt the pinch of hunger, and had pulled his belt in tighter than ever before.

The night fell crisp and clear. The temperature dropped. The half-starved coyotes were out early, their lonely singsong quavering on all sides. The rancher let his sheep dogs go hungry, since with empty stomachs they would keep a better watch.

Exhausted as he was, the hunted dog might have escaped that night. There were other ranches within a few miles. Up here they had not heard of a sheep-killing dog. Up here there were no night watches. He might have killed another sheep and gone away with new strength.

He was too scared and confused and lonely to dare this. Even before the lights went out in the little ranch house, he came limping down to it. He lay on his belly and yearned to go inside. In the morning they saw his tracks, where he had prowled around the house and then down toward the sheepsheds, where the faithful, hungry dogs had driven him off.

"I thought I heard them, but I sure never thought he'd have the nerve to come around!" said Walt Trescoli. "You've got to admire him. I wish this was over."

Bill Ehmken, studying the tracks and leading his horse, said nothing. He saw where the big dog had lain in the snow for hours, watching the house, until loneliness and hunger and the freezing cold

made him move on. Bill stared off at the horizon
for a long time.

"He's bleeding in one foot, Dwight," he said.

Dwight nodded.

"He's dead game," Bill went on, after a moment. "I wish there was some other way out. Well
. . . let's go."

They got into the saddle and pushed on.

Almost at once they saw the dog. He was lying
in the snow, less than a quarter of a mile ahead of
them, on the hillside. He was stretched out with his
nose pointed back along his own trail. He half
stood up when he saw them.

Bucky yanked out his gun and fired. The dog
broke and ran, giving one terrified yelp.

Joe Turnbull tore open his coat and ripped off
his badge. His limber pitcher's arm whirled, and
the silvery badge skimmed through the air. It fell
in the snow under Limpy, making the pinto shy.

"That's all for me," Joe yelled. "I'm through."

"Cut that out now," Bill Ehmken warned.

Joe turned his horse and shook his fist at Bill.
"I'm through with you too. What's fair about this?
What chance has he got? You know as well as I do
that the wolves got most of those sheep, but you're
too scared of what people will say. Well, I'm not.
I'm going home."

Bill looked both angry and ashamed. Dwight
leaned out of the saddle and picked up the badge.
He rode over and held it out to Joe.

"Put it back on. What good did that do you?"

Joe refused the badge at first. Then his shoulders slumped. He pinned it back on his coat.

"It did *me* some good," he said. "I feel better, anyway. I'm sorry, Bill."

Bill said nothing.

The dog was almost continuously in sight all day, although not once did they get within rifle range. He seemed to know by now just how far the guns would reach. He limped along just outside that deadly limit, his heavy head hanging.

"Keep firing," Bill said. "Let's get this over with."

Each time they fired, the dog burst into an awkward lope. He was favoring his sore foot more and more, and this threw an unnatural, jolting burden on the other three feet. These bursts of speed hurt his bleeding feet and swollen legs cruelly.

The posse had brought a few sandwiches from the ranch, but they did not stop to eat. They munched as they rode. The clear, cold afternoon wore on. The sun slanted downward toward the jagged Montana sky line. They were out of the Badlands now, in rolling sheep and cattle range where the brush was heavier and where a few trees grew. Bill pointed to a lonely little house off to the east.

"See that? That rancher owns range on both sides of the line, and his house is built right on the border," he said. "Beyond that is Canada. My dad used to take me hunting around here. We're a long way from home."

Dwight's heart began hammering unbearably.

All day he had ridden with a heavy weight in his chest. It lifted suddenly and a wild, crazy hope made him tremble. He pulled Limpy back to a stop.

"Wait a minute!" he cried.

Up ahead the dog had thrown himself down wearily in the snow. He was looking back toward them. He had put his big head down on his forepaws and his great tail was stretched out behind him. He looked immense.

"What's the matter?" said Bill.

"Then he's in Canada, isn't he?" Dwight said. "He made it across the line, didn't he?"

Bucky understood first. He shouted: "Have you lost your wits completely, Dwight? What difference does that line make to a sheep-killing dog? You talk like he's human."

Dwight faced them all, red-faced, not too sure of himself, but stubbornly determined.

"I don't care. I guess he's as good as some humans," he cried. "Is killing sheep worse than killing people? You wouldn't dare follow a murderer across that line. You'd let *him* get away, even if he killed your own flesh and blood. A murderer would get a fair trial, and all the mercy that the law allows—but that dog won't." Dwight was crying, this time not hopelessly, this time in excitement—and this time without caring who saw him cry.

"A man's supposed to know better, but a dog isn't. Well, you're not going to shoot anything. You put your gun away, Bucky. He made it across that line and he gets his chance, the same as a man would."

Bucky cocked his gun. The dog stood up.

"You wait till your dad hears about this. Get out of my way, boy!"

Bill reached for the old bachelor's arm.

"Just a minute, there," he said sharply. "I'm still giving the orders. We could get into a peck of trouble, taking a posse across an international border."

"To kill a sheep-killing dog?" Bucky yelled.

"To kill anything," said Bill. "Suppose the dog's owner turns up, Bucky? Suppose he files suit up there. Suppose he gets up in front of a Canadian jury and says that dog was worth five or six thousand dollars—any price he wants to name. What do you think a Canadian jury is going to do to an American posse that violates the border?"

No one said anything for a moment. Then Emil Hoffman sighed: "I know what an American jury would do, and I haven't got that kind of money. Here's where I stop."

"Me too," said Walt Trescoli. "I just work for a living. I don't want any trouble with the law."

"Besides, fair is fair!" Joe cried. "What kind of man are you, Uncle Bucky?"

"Think it over, Bucky," Deputy Bill pleaded. "If a man made in God's own image can commit a crime against God and man and escape across that line, then surely this poor, simple creature has the same right. Some man got him into this trouble, by turning him loose in a sheep country without explaining the laws of a sheep country to him. No one told him about the Canadian line, either, when it comes to that.

"But if one kind of unknown law can get him into trouble, another kind can give him a second chance. Dwight's been against us all along, and how many of you have ever known Dwight to be wrong about an animal? I say the boy and the dog both have earned a second chance. What do you say, Bucky? You're a fair man."

Bucky hesitated. Dwight slid out of the saddle and handed his reins to Joe. He began uncoiling the rope from his saddle horn.

Again Bucky was the first to understand.

"Maybe I can't chase him into Canada," he said, "but you bring that dog back into North Dakota, and he's the deadest dog you ever saw, boy."

No one else said anything. Dwight walked forward, carrying the rope.

Bucky half raised the rifle.

"Give the kid a chance, Bucky," said Bill. "Just watch. You're going to see something you'll remember all the rest of your life."

Slowly, old Bucky lowered his rifle.

174

Dwight walked forward, dragging the rope, his wild half quivering as a wild thing quivers at the unexpected kind touch of a man. The big, gaunt, red-eyed dog watched Dwight's every move. He trembled, as though to run.

"Down!"

The dog sank down, giving up his freedom forever. Dwight's heart gave a proud leap. He had been right, and the others wrong, all along. There was no mistake now.

He slapped his leg with his hand and said, "Come here, boy."

The dog crept forward an inch at a time, slinking along on his belly with his tail between his legs. Closer and closer he came, until his massive head lay on the toes of Dwight's boots.

Dwight leaned down and put his rope around the dog's neck. The dog licked his face and whimpered. He turned over on his back to show how completely he had surrendered. Dwight dropped to his knees and threw his arm around the big, shaggy neck.

"My dog, my dog!" he whispered.

CHAPTER THIRTEEN

"OH, NO, NOT ANOTHER BIG DOG!" Mrs. Jerome wailed.

"Please, Mom, wait till you get to know him," Dwight pleaded.

"I don't want to know him," Mrs. Jerome said firmly. She liked small, fluffy dogs, and not too many of them. She stared at the big mutt as he came out of the car with his tail between his legs. "Oh, dear, he isn't really a dog. Why, he's so huge!"

"Don't be afraid, Mom," said Dwight. "Look, he wouldn't hurt a flea."

He had already learned that people found it hard to believe their eyes, when first they saw the dog. "As big as a yearling colt," Vaughn Jacobs had said. "As big as a horse," Bucky Turnbull grumbled, after sharing the back seat with Dwight and Joe and the dog for fifty long miles.

A crowd had gathered at the Jeromes' this Sunday afternoon, to see the captive unloaded. At every filling station and roadside ranch along the road home people had waited to stop the car and

see the big mutt for themselves. It was Deputy
Bill's idea to telephone ahead and have people
prepared, and it had proved wise.

The posse had spent the previous night at the
little ranch up on the border. Dwight slept in the
hay barn with the chained dog stretched out beside
his blankets. When Bill looked in in the morning
he found the boy and the dog crowded close
together. The hay barn reeked with the carbolic
salves Dwight had smeared on the dog's sore
feet.

The dog looked up at Bill and rustled his tail in
the hay, but he was careful not to awaken
Dwight.

Watching them, Bill knew that a long, weary
time of heartbreak was over for Dwight. But he
knew sheepmen, and another might be starting. He
went back into the house and put in a call for
Sheriff Lang to tell him that the long hunt was at
last over.

"That's what you think," said the sheriff.

Bill, at the time, paid no attention to this re-
mark. "Send up a truck for the horses and gear," he
said. "The fellow we're staying with will bring us
home as soon as Dwight and Joe wake up. They're
played out. We'll be home about noon, dog and
all.

"Because I'm letting Dwight keep it, Cecil. I
wish you'd pass the word so people can have their
fits and get over them. This boy has had enough
trouble about this. He tried to do things our way,

even knowing we were wrong. Now I'm going to see that his way gets a fair chance."

"Sure, Bill. Things couldn't be much worse, anyway." The sheriff sounded unhappy, but still Bill did not notice. "I knew you'd never kill that dog," the old man went on, "and I didn't want you to."

"Then why—?" the astonished Bill began.

"Oh, I have my own way of doing things. I'll meet you at Clay Jerome's place. I suppose you'd like to have me bring Laura Stevenson along."

"Well, if it's not too much trouble, Cecil. . . ."

Now Dwight was too excited about being home at last, too worried about the big dog's reception, to think it was queer so many people were here. Miss Stevenson's eyes were shining with unshed tears. Vaughn Jacobs looked sober, but not at all upset. Both Haberstrohs were here, with their big families. Old Arnold Hoffman had driven over to bring Emil home.

"I hope you know what you're doing, Dwight," said Mr. Jerome. "Bring him into the house and let's see how he behaves. I think he's been a house dog at one time."

"Girls, stay away from him!" Mrs. Jerome cried.

But she was too late. Irene and Christine and Trinket had thrown themselves on the big dog. He cringed and looked up at Dwight.

"It's all right," Dwight said, scratching the dog's ear. "Behave!"

The dog seemed uncomfortable, with so many eyes staring at him, but he wagged his tail and ran his big, wet tongue over Trinket's face.

"What's his name? What are you going to call him? Can we name him?" the girls begged.

Dwight had given considerable thought to a name for his dog. So far, none of them seemed to fit.

"Well, what would you call him?"

"Lead! Let's call him Lead," the girls cried.

They had already agreed on this name. The Jerome children, Dwight included, had never tired of hearing their father tell about the dogs he had known or owned, first as a sheepman's son, then as a sheepman himself. Of all these, a sable collie named Lead had been his favorite. Many long winter evenings had been passed with tales of Lead's wisdom and devotion and courage. The old collie had lived to the age of sixteen, and then drowned in a spring flood, trying to bring a lamb to safety long after he was too old and stiff to swim.

"Lead," said Dwight. "Lead. All right, Lead it is." The dog fitted the name and the name fitted the dog.

"You're not going to gain anything, trying to get on my soft side," Mr. Jerome warned, opening the door. "He's got to earn his way, and he's got to let the sheep alone. One mistake, Dwight, and he's through."

The crowd filed in after the dog. Colleen got up

from behind the stove and growled her fierce threats. Dwight spoke to her sharply.

"Behave, Colleen. Lie down, Lead."

The big mutt slunk to a corner behind the stove and dropped to the floor thankfully. The wolf-hound stopped growling, but it was plain she did not approve of taking the truant into the house.

"He's had training," Mr. Jerome said. "That's a good start."

"Let's take him down to the sheepshed and see how he gets along with Patch," said Dwight.

Mr. Jerome hesitated. "There isn't any Patch," he said. "The wolves got him night before last. I wasn't gone more than fifteen minutes. Just went up for more coal, and before I got back they'd killed Patch and dragged out a sheep. Got him before I could get down there.

"And last night they got one of Vaughn's dogs and two more of his sheep. Vaughn wasn't gone more than fifteen minutes, either. It seems to be the same pair of wolves. Vaughn and I ran one pair down and shot them, but there's another pair still working. You're not going to have much time to fool with your new dog, Dwight. You and Bill are going to have to get this pair of cruisers."

"Because," said the sheriff, "someday they're not going to wait for the man to turn his back. Some-time they'll be hungry and desperate enough to jump the man. I don't want to hear any more talk about sheep-killing dogs from anyone. Is that clear?

The dogs are all that stand between you people and ruin."

Mr. Jerome turned to look out of the window. Dwight knew how his father loved the sheep dogs, and how guilty he felt to have a third one lay down its life for him in a single winter. Mr. Jerome's low voice was calm enough, but that didn't fool Dwight.

"When the history of this greatest of all storms is written, let no one forget the heroism of the sheep dogs of the West. We know what they've done for us, and we're just a small corner of the land covered by this storm. All over the range country dogs have died this way, cut up by wolves and coyotes and lions, frozen with their flocks, smothered by drifts, starved when they could have come in without their sheep.

"In every county in the West there will be these stories of heroism and devotion, to be told and retold around the family fireside for years to come. We won't build any memorials to the gallant dogs who laid down their lives in this storm. Well then, let these warm little family tales be their monument!

"Let them be told again and again to our children, and to our children's children, and to their children after them. Loyalty is all too scarce in this world of ours today, and each generation must learn over again that life isn't worth living unless it's worth dying for too. We have never needed more this lesson of simple, sturdy faith and bravery.

"That's why I want to give this mongrel of Dwight's a second chance, for Patch and Feistie and Wrangle, who died for me and mine. Maybe I can make it up to them a little bit, by showing kindness to another dog. Maybe God keeps track of such things. We can't go on in this world, just taking and taking, never giving anything in return. I'd like to give back just a small part of the loyalty that Patch and Feistie and Wrangle gave to me, and I hope my neighbors will bear with me."

Bill said quickly, "Dwight, will that big mutt track a wolf, do you think?"

"I know he will."

Bill looked up at Mr. Jerome. Now he understood the sheriff's gloomy conversation over the phone.

"There's your answer, Clay. Let this dog rest his sore feet a few days, and get some weight on him, while Dwight and I scout around and try to find where this pair of cruisers is denned up. Then let this boy and his dog have a chance."

Mr. Jerome nodded. "First, let's take him down to the sheep and teach him to let them alone while he's still new here, and eager to please. He's got to learn to obey me too, while Dwight's away. The rest of you stay here, and let Dwight and me take him down."

The trusting sheep ignored the big dog as Dwight led him into the warm, pungently scented shed. As for the dog, he knew too well that sheep meant trouble. He thought he was going to be punished for his misdeeds, and Dwight had to speak to him sharply to make him follow.

He chained the big mutt to a post in the center of the flock and sat down with his father at the other end of the shed. The sheep approached the dog curiously. He cringed back and growled at them.

"No, Lead!" Dwight said. "No, no!"

The dog quivered, not quite understanding. An old ewe pressed close to him, nuzzling his bony ribs curiously. He growled again.

"No, Lead. Down!"

The dog lay down with a patient grunt. He seemed to find this a lot of foolishness, but if that's what it took to please this boy, it was all right with him. He was a one-man dog, and he had found his man. He was Dwight's dog forever, and Dwight was his man.

He ignored the sheep and licked his sore paws, flapping his long tongue peevishly at the rank carbolic taste of the salve. All their lives these sheep had been cared for by some dog. They could not remember life without a dog—if, indeed, they could remember anything for more than a minute or two. They crowded closer and closer as Lead's strange smell quickly became familiar to them.

The sheep adopted him long before he adopted them. He was their dog, and they were his sheep, forever.

The bewildered dog got up and turned around several times, as though wondering why these crazy things insisted on crowding him when there was so much room everywhere. Each time Dwight or his father spoke firmly. Each time the dog lay down again, and each time the sheep moved closer and closer.

The dog, licking at his feet, felt the warm breath of the curious old ewe in his face. He raised his head, and this time he knew better than to growl. They touched noses, while Dwight and his father held their breath. The dog's odd hound ears shot forward, as he got acquainted with sheep that were merely sheep, and not meat.

Down went his head. He stretched out, as best he could under the circumstances, and put his massive head between his paws. His ears drooped. His eyes closed. The old ewe rested her neck across his back and began chewing her cud.

"I guess we can leave him now," said Mr. Jerome.

Not all at once did the dog learn his new duties. For one thing, he was in bad physical condition. The lean week in the Badlands with Colleen, followed by that cruel chase ahead of the posse, had taken a grim toll of his great strength. For a long time, he was content just to lie in the warm, dry shed, resting and sleeping. The bright part of his day was early in the morning, when the three girls brought him his food before going to school.

He always came to the end of his chain to meet them, and the only time he barked was when, in the morning, he heard the slam of the back door, the shrill voices and laughter that meant the girls were coming.

He missed Dwight, who was out each day with Deputy Bill. There was no school for Dwight, no time to waste on the dog, which was left in Mr. Jerome's charge for training. Loneliness, as much as anything else, taught Lead his new job. It gave him something to occupy his restless brute mind.

In sheep dogs with the ancient collie strain, the brooding tenderness for sheep is a thing inborn. Lead was a hunter, designed to track down game with his keen nose and then kill it in close combat. The fierce protective instinct that made sheep more important than life to a collie was absent in him. But he was left alone with the sheep, hour after hour, until he got used to having them around. They were his only company, and soon they became his friends.

Little by little he came to understand how precious sheep were in this household. Even without the collie's herd instinct, he soon would have fought for the sheep, just as he would have fought for anything belonging to the Jeromes. This was his home now. Let trespassers beware! Even Colleen, who never could learn about sheep, was not welcome in the sheepshed after a while.

He learned how to handle sheep—learned that while one loud bark scattered them, another quickly brought them together, where he or Mr. Jerome wanted them. He learned, above all, patience, the eternal patience that must be the rule with sheep, or they run and crowd and refuse to eat, and die. He never snapped at a sheep, but for a while, until taught not to, he slapped at them with his powerful forepaws when he became annoyed at the silly creatures. This great Dane trick was no light punishment, and had to be stopped, for he could bowl a sheep over with a blow.

But another Dane trait proved helpful and gave promise that he might someday be an excellent sheep dog.

"He's got Dane blood in him, that's sure," Mr. Jerome reported to Dwight. "I've heard that some Danes think of themselves as people and want to have cats or other dogs as pets of their own. I never quite believed this until I saw Lead making pets of the sheep.

"He doesn't exactly love them as a born sheep dog would, but he seems to think they're his, and he likes to boss them around. He wants them *where* he wants them, *when* he wants them. He's annoyed when they do foolish things and proud when they behave well. It's all new, but he's learning."

Mr. Jerome thought a moment, and then went on: "He's a city dog, and I don't suppose the jungle is any harder on its wild animals than the city is on its dogs. Only the very strong, the very swift, the very smart, can survive the hard life on the hard pavements.

"That's why so many mongrels seem smarter than expensive purebreds. Any grown dog picked up off the streets *has* to be smart, or he wouldn't be alive. Lead had that kind of life. He's the pick of thousands and thousands of alley mongrels, and he'll do, he'll do!"

The dog's hardest lesson was to get over his terror of firearms. But Mr. Jerome was firm and patient, and at last Lead learned to ignore a gun, even when it was fired over his head. He cringed only when a gun barrel was pointed at him. To this extent, he would never forget the lesson the dead-eyed Walt had taught him.

Every day Dwight and Bill were out, but the wolves knew they were being pursued, and by now they knew how to hide their trails. The old tracks always led up into the Badlands. There were no really new ones. Dwight and Bill found plenty of wolf sign, but it was all cold. Again and again Dwight got out of the saddle to study the fading legend in the snow. Again and again he stood up wearily, saying: "Several days old, but better than nothing. Shall we try it?"

"We might as well." Bill too was always tired.

They found where the pair of wolves had killed rabbits, and where they had prowled close to sheepsheds, and where they had dug out a coyote and eaten it, in their starved desperation. In his mind, Dwight came to see them clearly, after endless days of following their cold trails. He was satisfied now, and so was Bill, that this pair was the last left in the country. They were too weak from hunger, or too well pleased with the fat pickings in the sheepsheds, to want to migrate. Death grew closer and closer, and they clung to life with boldness and savage cunning, each day learning some new trick of survival under man's very nose.

It was queer how little Dwight and Bill had to say to each other in these long days in the saddle. Bill did not seem to care about the picture of the wolves that Dwight was gradually putting together in his mind as he followed the cold trails. Something was missing; Dwight's old friend had changed. Dwight talked this over with his father.

"Of course he's changed," Mr. Jerome chuckled. "So will you. That's part of growing up. Bill's engaged to be married, and he'd rather be with his girl than with you. He'll spend more and more time carrying in the wash, less and less time hunting and fishing with you, I'm thinking. But if you ever need a friend, I guess you'll know where to find one."

"Well-l-l-l, I guess so," said Dwight.

Now that he thought about it, it seemed that some of his own wildness was leaving him. He was glad to get home each night, so he could read and study. He was less eager to saddle Limpy and ride out in the cold each morning. He found himself thinking more and more of spring, and of getting out his big catcher's mitt so that Joe Turnbull could warm up his "business arm."

Dwight had just gone to bed one evening when he heard the phone ring. His father came to the trap door that led to the attic and called him. Dwight went down and answered sleepily.

"Hello."

It was Deputy Bill, and his voice crackled with excitement.

"Dwight, saddle up as quickly as you can and get over to Nils Haberstroh's. Bring the big outlaw dog with you. Nils was attacked by a wolf just about an hour ago. His arm and hand are hurt, I don't know how badly. We've got a fresh trail. Now let's see what that big dog of yours can do with it."

Mr. Jerome rode to the Haberstroh ranch with Dwight. Lead was glad of a chance to run, and he seemed to feel the excitement. He kept up with the galloping horses without urging.

They found Deputy Bill waiting for them. They tarried just long enough to hear what had happened. Nils would live. His hand and arm were ripped to the bone, and he was white and weak from loss of blood, but worst of all was the shock of fright and horror. It was something he would never forget.

Nils had partitioned off a little bunk room in his long sheepshed, using canvas haystack covers for walls. Here he had been spending his nights, on guard. Tonight he had been sitting on the edge of his bunk, mending harness by lantern light, getting ready for spring plowing. The sheep were bedded down in the other end of the shed, the collie among them.

"I thought I heard the dog yelp once," Nils said weakly. "I guess that was his last sound. They just cut him in two."

A few minutes later, he heard what he thought was a strange dog growling. He ran out to investigate, carrying his lantern and a heavy leather harness tug.

The collie was dead, killed almost in complete silence within a hundred yards of where Nils had been sitting. He saw where a dead sheep had been dragged boldly across the corral. It still lay next to the woven wire fence. There the "dog" had been unable to drag it farther. There, dimly, Nils saw not just one "dog," but two.

He ran toward them, shouting and brandishing the leather tug. One leaped the fence. The other turned and sprang at Nils. He saw slanting eyes that glowed yellowly in the light of his lantern, and he knew that this was no dog.

He dropped the lantern and screamed, instinctively throwing an arm across his face. He was knocked backward by the silent ferocity of the attack, but he managed to twist. He fell face downward in the snow, half stunned.

Strangely, the wolf did not follow up the attack. Nils raised his head. There, almost within reach of his feet, were both wolves, tearing at the carcass of the dead sheep.

He stood it as long as he could, hearing their ravenous whimpers. The fallen lantern smoked, sputtered . . . and went out. Nils leaped to his feet and ran to the house, screaming.

Deputy Bill's flashlight showed that the wolves had taken their time.

"Nils got off lucky, but the next man had better carry a gun," he said. "What's the matter with Lead? He's not even interested."

"He knows what he's doing," said Dwight.

The big dog seemed barely curious as he snuffed around the bloody snow. But when Dwight unsnapped the chain from his collar, Lead sailed over the fence and vanished into the darkness, running hard. In a moment his deep, bell-like trail voice broke the silence. There was a throbbing sound to it that made Dwight's heart pound.

They ran to their horses, piled into the saddle, and followed as best they could, stumbling through drifts and ditches and gates, relying on their horses when they themselves could not see. On and on that deep, throbbing hunter's cry called them.

Then suddenly there was silence. They reined in and listened.

"He's lost the trail," Dwight said disappointedly. "They've fooled him, someway."

In a little while they heard Lead again, but he was only barking peevishly. They followed the sound and found him coursing up and down the paved highway.

Here the trail was broken. Again and again he came back to where it ended, but it was not until long after daylight that Dwight figured out what had happened, and picked up the other end.

The wolves had jumped the pavement to run along the other edge awhile. Then they had crossed again—and again, and again, and again. The confusion of scents on this, the only through road in the country, helped hide theirs. Finally they had leaped the railing of the bridge where Dwight had killed those other two wolves, and here Lead picked up the cold trail.

He followed it deep into the Badlands, but with considerable difficulty, since it grew colder and colder. It was nearly midnight when Dwight called the big mutt back, put him on the chain, and went home. The tired dog dropped down amidst his sheep with a thankful grunt.

It was a long time before either Dwight or his father could sleep that night. They kept seeing Nils Haberstroh's white, staring face, the fright and horror in his eyes. Dwight's last thought was, *I'll get those wolves if it's the last thing I do. . . .*

CHAPTER FOURTEEN

"YOU MAY AS WELL GO BACK TO SCHOOL," Bill said a few days later. "I'll call you if I need you. Just let me have that big dog now and then."

So Dwight went back to school, and Bill prowled the country alone on his horse. Now and then he came to get Lead, but each time the trail was so cold that the dog had trouble following it from the first.

Always the scent was broken at the highway. The wolves had learned to use it, much as some hunted animals use a running stream. They hid their scent in a confusion of scents—cars and horses and cattle, dogs and cats and human beings, as well as countless bold coyotes that traveled there.

Scarcely a week passed but what some fresh outrage was reported. Apparently the wolves singled out a ranch and watched it, night after night, just out of range of the sheep dogs' keen noses. A sheepman needed to turn his back only a moment to have dead dogs, dead sheep.

Sometimes he heard the savage scuffle, sometimes he did not. Sometimes he saw one or both of the lean, sable-and-gray forms flashing away through the darkness. Sometimes when he came back there was only a dead dog, the stained snow, and the torn carcass across the corral, where the wolves had dragged a sheep.

No one forgot Nils Haberstroh and his bandages. No one left the house after dark without a cocked gun.

Spring comes late to North Dakota. Long after spring floods were running in the Black Hills a few hundred miles to the south, winter kept its hard fist locked on the Badlands. Ranchers dug deeper and deeper into their dwindling grain and hay supplies, and hoped they would last.

But the work horses knew that spring was near. They had rested a long time, and now they frisked and fought as they took their turns at the heated water tanks in the morning. They leaned against fences and scratched their shaggy winter coats, eager to be rid of them.

In their tunneled avenues below the frost line, the prairie dogs and ground squirrels and gophers knew it was time for spring. They made their underground cities neat. The winter's dead were buried, sealed off in tunnels that never would be used again. In other pocketed rooms in the populous earth, this year's newborn millions squirmed and squeaked in darkness, waiting for the light.

It was a time of birth for the coyotes too, but cold and famine had been hard on these sly little prairie pilferers. The litters were smaller this year, with one or two whelps instead of five or six. Even these small families went hungry and became smaller as the hard-working old he-coyotes found hunting poor and risky.

It was the spring miracle of birth that told the sheepmen too that spring was at hand. They stopped grumbling about snowdrifts. Heavy drifts meant more water in the earth and more grass for their lambs. The storm that had brought famine and suffering to the old year meant abundance for the new. Thus nature again struck that balance which Mr. Jerome talked about. It took away here, and gave back there.

At first there was only a lamb now and then, born early and out of season. "More trouble than they're worth," the sheepmen said; yet nothing was too much trouble, if it helped the first lambs to live.

A few hundred miles to the south, people were saying excitedly, "I saw a robin today!"

The robins were still a month away from North Dakota; but one evening Mr. Jerome came home and said: "Bucky's got his first orphan lamb in a box behind the stove. And I saw Emil Hoffman in town. Two of their ewes have lambed. It seems to me they're starting early this year."

Each spring, sheepmen said, "It seems to me they're starting early this year."

And then the lambing season was on them. Again Dwight put aside his books, and so did every child old enough to lend a hand in this busiest of sheepmen's seasons. There was no rest, day or night—but especially no rest at night.

Dwight and his father scarcely left the dope room and the sheepshed. Their meals were brought to them. They took turns sleeping, and sometimes they forgot to sleep altogether.

Anyone who thought the sheepmen were brutal when they clubbed coyotes to death on the wolf drag should have seen their tenderness with the lambs. Bucky was not the only sheepman who nursed orphans in his living room behind the stove.

To Dwight, it sometimes seemed that a ewe was the only mother on earth who would drive her own baby away at birth, to starve for all she cared. He would no sooner make up his mind that all sheep were bad mothers than one would butt him headlong, merely for daring to walk too close to her lamb.

Stupid, weak, helpless, prey to disease and to every meat-eating animal on earth, sheep are a problem to the sheepman from birth to death, but never more than at birth.

Some ewes died, leaving orphaned lambs. Other ewes bleated in endless sorrow for their own dead lambs, yet refused to adopt the little orphans. Their stupidity gave the sheepman his chance to trick them. There was no time to experiment, to see if perhaps *this* particular ewe might not take *that* particular lamb. The orphans died too quickly, unless warmed and fed. Their thin baby bleating grew thinner with each passing minute, and they literally cried themselves to death.

As soon as a lamb was found dead, Dwight's father pushed the grieving mother aside and skinned the dead baby. While he was doing this, Dwight brought one of the waifs from the orphan pen. The skin of the dead one was tied around the orphan like an extra coat. Dressed in his borrowed skin, the hungry little orphan was then put beside the bereaved mother, with a pinch on the ear to make it cry.

Usually the mother caught the scent of her dead baby, now miraculously come to life. She charged to its defense when it cried out, too upset to realize that she was being duped. Having "rescued" the lamb from Dwight and his father, she cared for it tenderly. So there was one more orphan that would not have to be kept behind the dope room stove, and fed from a bottle.

The skins of the dead lambs fell off, or were taken off, in a few hours or days. By then, the ewe and lamb thought they had always belonged to each other. But this was a solution to only one problem.

There were some little orphans that never were adopted. For some reason known only to the sheep, they were rejected again and again. These became pets of the girls, whose job it was to make "formula" and feed the little outcasts. From pets they would quickly grow to be pests. They did not want to go out to grass with the other sheep, and the other sheep did not want them. There was always trouble when first these bottle babies were turned in with the flock.

The headlong charge of a frisky orphan lamb is amusing, and a small girl can hold it with her outstretched skirt. The same charge, when the orphan has grown to weigh a hundred pounds a few months later, can be a dangerous nuisance. From first to last, the bottle babies were trouble. The girls cried with broken hearts when finally these orphans were hauled over to market, but Dwight and his father heaved sighs of relief.

Then there were mothers with too much mother instinct, instead of too little. They neglected their own babies in their efforts to steal lambs from other ewes. Sometimes they stole five or six before they were caught at it. Then the shed rang with an angry, sorrowful bleating, until Dwight and his father sorted out the kidnapped babies and returned them, as best they could, to their rightful mothers.

Sometimes the mothers took the truants back, but sometimes they caught the scent of the strange ewe on them and would have nothing to do with their own children. One ewe caused endless difficulty this spring. Her babies were black, and she thought every black lamb born this year belonged to her. She had her own two, and four more whose mothers positively refused to take them back, before in desperation Dwight separated them all from the flock.

All six lambs became, in part, bottle babies. The ewe did not have milk enough to feed them all, and she refused to let the girls come near. Dwight and his father had to give the lambs their bottles, and still the old ewe complained bitterly whenever she saw, through the fence, a black lamb with another mother.

Wherever Dwight went, the dog tried to go. His chain let him pad back and forth, up and down, following the tired, sleepy boy as he plodded on his rounds. Whenever Dwight walked past with a small lamb in his arms, the dog trotted along beside him, rubbing his leg, rearing himself to sniff curiously at the lamb. When he came to the end of his chain he stood wagging his tail until Dwight returned that way later. He liked this company, this work, this excitement. Being a sheepman's dog was far, far better than being a New York dog.

Over fifteen hundred lambs were born on the Jerome ranch in a space of less than thirty days. Most of them came in the ten hours between nightfall and morning. This was an average of better than five births an hour. It meant endless, grueling work while it lasted, but between any father and son who shared this hard and tender labor there was a deep bond that grew deeper. The families of sheepmen are not split with ugly quarrels.

For sheepmen have been doing this work since Biblical times; and what Dwight and his father did, the Old Testament prophets had done long before them. From their foolish, stupid, wayward, helpless sheep, Dwight and his father learned patience and tolerance for their fellow men, who also often were foolish, stupid, wayward, and helpless.

Better than most people, Dwight understood the Twenty-third Psalm. It had been sung by shepherd boys like himself, boys who had struggled through many a long, weary night saving orphaned lambs and mourning mothers—boys who knew the need for goodness and mercy, as only sheepmen's sons may know it.

It was a hard life, a lonely life, but Dwight wanted no other. The sheepman is by nature lonely. He lives on land too worthless and too sparsely green for any other useful purpose. He abides with the weather, which can change from friend to foe and back to friend again in the twinkling of an eye. Simple are his wants, simple his food, plain his bed, small and modest his house. His hand is gentle on the beasts he owns. Self-reliantly he lives, and continuously in peace; for when a man's greatest worries are green pastures and still waters, he has less time than most men for causing trouble, and less heart for it.

This is what it meant to be a sheepman's son. This was why Dwight had helped hunt down the big outlaw mutt, though it broke his heart to do it.

Father and son worked together, while the big dog loafed on his chain and grew fat, while Colleen spent more and more time building a nest in the coalpit, while down in the earth the little squirming things grew restless, and spring lurked around every corner.

Then the storm struck again.

One last, murderous blizzard came down out of the Athabasca country. For three days and nights the snow fell, the wind howled. The school, always half empty during the lambing season, closed altogether. Miss Stevenson made one last trip back to Minneapolis, and her train east was the last to run for several days.

On the fourth night the storm died, and the moon came out bright and clear. But thousands of cattle and sheep, lured out by the premature spring elsewhere, were caught in fresh drifts. Death losses mounted all over the West as heartsick ranchers sought vainly to haul feed to starving herds and flocks cut off by the storm. In desperation, baled hay and bagged grain were dropped from Air Force bombers. New roads were cut to trains stalled between towns, and not for two or three weeks did some towns again have rail and road and telephone connections with the outside world.

Again an unbroken mantle of fresh snow stretched from the Texas Panhandle to the Arctic Circle, and nowhere was it heavier than in the North Dakota Badlands. Yet here there had been no spring to trick people; here they were still dug in, fighting their eternal war against winter and cold and snow and wind.

On the Jerome ranch there was contentment. One morning father and son looked at each other and knew that the lambing season was over, as suddenly as it had begun. A few more might be born, but these would be easily cared for. The sheepshed was quiet at last. The silly old ewes chewed their cuds and watched their offspring proudly. The lambs that had been so weak now were strong and nimble. They would live.

Mr. Jerome yawned, and smiled at his son.

"Go up to the house and have a hot bath, and go to bed," he said. "Sleep around the clock. Don't worry about me! I won't be far behind you."

"All right, Dad."

Dwight gave Lead one last pat, and went up to the house. It was not quite five in the morning, and still quite dark, when he crawled into bed in his attic room. It was like coming home after a long, long trip, to feel these familiar warm covers about him once more.

The next thing he knew it was broad daylight, and his father was shaking him and saying: "Wake up, Dwight. Wake up, wake up."

Dwight sat up and rubbed his eyes. Something in his father's face was frightening.

"What's wrong?" he cried.

"I'm afraid we're in a peck of trouble. Lead got away, and Bucky and Joe Turnbull are downstairs.

Bucky had two sheep killed during the night, and probably a lamb was stolen too."

Dwight jumped out of bed, shaking his sleepy head angrily. "I don't believe it. I mean, maybe he lost some sheep, but Lead didn't kill them."

"We'll see," the father said. "Joe claims he recognized his tracks in the snow. I hate this! Bucky's being pretty decent about it, but we'll never live it down if we've turned a sheep killer loose on the country again."

"I don't care what he says or what Joe saw, it wasn't Lead," Dwight said stubbornly.

He dressed quickly and went downstairs. Joe and Bucky were waiting uncomfortably in the living room.

"I was afraid of this, Dwight," said old Bucky. "Once a sheep killer, always a sheep killer, but I knew how much store you set by that dog and I wanted him to have his fair chance."

Joe was taking it hard too. "It's as much my fault as yours, Dwight," he said.

Dwight would have felt better if Bucky had come over here raging and storming. He could hear his sisters crying in the kitchen. They had not had much chance to get acquainted with Lead, but they loved all dogs, and they were proud of the ex-outlaw.

Dwight put his coat on as he went out the door, carrying the Arisaka.

"How about wolves?" he asked.

"I'm no expert," said Bucky, "and the way the

sheep had milled around I had trouble finding any tracks inside the corral. Outside the fence is where we saw the dog's sign. I'm sorry, Dwight, but I don't think there's much chance of a mistake."

"You wait and see," Dwight said. "How did Lead get away, Dad?"

"I don't know. I fell asleep in the dope room right after you went up to the house. I don't know when he got away. He just pulled his head through the collar and slipped out."

"You wait and see, he didn't do it. If he did, I'll kill him myself," said Dwight.

"And I'll buy him a bucketful of beefsteak if he didn't," said Bucky. "That's a promise."

The two Turnbulls had come in Bucky's car. By the time Dwight and his father had their horses saddled, the two were out of sight. Colleen came out of the coalpit, but she did not coax to go along.

When they got to Bucky's, the old man and his nephew were waiting with their own saddled horses beside the corral, beside a dead sheep. Another lay a few feet away. Dwight slid out of the saddle and turned one of the frozen carcasses over. He didn't need to look very close. The way Limpy was acting told him all he wanted to know. The pinto smelled wolf!

"See, Dad, does that look like the work of that big-jawed dog to you? This sheep was slashed to death, wolf style. I'll show you. Maybe you can't pick out the wolf tracks from Lead's, but I can.

"Sure, Lead was here—but not after sheep. I know my dog. Well, this trail ought to be easy to follow. Let's go."

It led them straight north into the Badlands. Soon it became clear, even to Bucky and Joe, that more than one animal had been running here. Soon they came to a dead lamb. Dwight did not even dismount.

"One of the wolves carried it this far," he said. "He probably dropped it when he heard Lead on his trail. You can see that Lead didn't even stop . . . or at least I can see it. Didn't anyone hear the dog baying trail?"

All three shook their heads.

"I wouldn't have heard the roof fall in," said Bucky. "I was catching up on a month of lost sleep."

"So was I," said Dwight, "but Lead wasn't."

He knew what had happened, as surely as if he had been there. He had seen the mutt fight wolves. He had seen him "mothering" the lambs, making pets of them in his clumsy great Dane way. The wind had brought him either the scent or the sound of the wolves. Unable to wake the tired, sleeping man in the dope room, he had done the only thing he could do.

The tracks were easy to follow in this bright sunlight. They loped on for nearly an hour. The trail curved to the west here, and the Jerome ranch came briefly into view and then was lost as they rode into the deeply scarred and drifted Badlands.

Mr. Jerome said: "I hope they didn't get your dog, Dwight. He's crowding them pretty close, and they're crafty fighters."

Dwight smiled. "You've never seen him fight wolves. I have."

"I wish I had your faith."

Dwight's eyes, roving farther and farther ahead, caught a dark spot in the snow. He stood up in the stirrups and pointed.

"There's one of them!" he cried, prodding Limpy into a gallop. And, a moment later: "There's the other one! He got both of them! Here, hold my horse, Joe, while I try to figure out what happened."

Limpy fought the reins, and could not be brought close to the dead wolves. The two killers lay less than a hundred yards apart, and the snow was roughed and reddened for yards around. Mr. Jerome dismounted too. The boy and his father went from wolf to wolf, while Bucky and Joe watched and listened in the saddle.

One thing was certain—it had been a battle, and a big one. It took more than savage, brute brawn to win that kind of fight. It took brains. It took courage. It took the kind of cleverness that could be learned only from man. Remembering how the dog had fought those other wolves, Dwight saw clearly what had happened.

"See, the wolves slowed down here, knowing

Lead was getting close, and that they were far enough from any house so they could fight him without being heard. They separated and tried to come at him from both sides—and I've seen them do that before.

"But he wasn't having any of it. Here's where he turned and ran, pretending he was heading for home as fast as he could go. Here's where the she-wolf got too eager, outrunning her mate. Here's where he turned and grabbed her. She realizes she's alone. She tries to get away. He didn't take time to finish her off, because her mate was too close. He just crippled her as best he could, and turned on the he-wolf.

"But the he-wolf doesn't want that kind of fight. See what's happening? He's running here, with the dog after him. The she-wolf can't keep up. Here's where the male tried to circle back. Here's where Lead cut him off and closed with him, and then broke off the fight when the she-wolf attacked from behind.

"Here's where they both try to run again, only Lead cut the crippled she-wolf down from behind—hurt her still more—then jumped the he-wolf again—hurt him still more. They didn't get to close with him until he was ready—until he'd cut them down to size.

"Now, here's where the she-wolf turned to fight it out, because she was badly hurt and couldn't do anything else. He finished her off here—shook her to death by the throat—choked her and probably broke her neck, and left her dead while he ran down the he-wolf and killed him here. I know.

"Because I've seen him fight them before. He wouldn't need two lessons. He's smart! I know how he'd do it because I've seen him, I've seen him. That's what I kept telling you all the time—I saw him fight wolves, and I know, I know."

Bucky looked down at the two dead wolves and shuddered as he thought of Nils Haberstroh and his mangled arm. He looked up at Dwight.

"You can make all this out by the tracks?" he said, a little doubtfully, as though reluctant to believe his own eyes.

"By the tracks, and because I've seen him fight wolves," Dwight insisted. "I tell you I know!"

"Then where's your dog now?"

"Home with his sheep, where he knows he belongs," Dwight said confidently.

Bucky glanced at Mr. Jerome, who smiled.

"There's a boy's faith for you, Bucky."

Bucky nodded thoughtfully. "What's the saying about a mustard seed? We could use a little of that ourselves."

Mr. Jerome laughed. "You never come to see us any more, except to complain about one of Dwight's dogs. You owe us just a nice, sociable visit. Let's go have a cup of the wife's coffee . . . and what'll you bet we find Lead right where Dwight says he is?"

"I'm not betting," said Bucky. "I already owe somebody a bucketful of beefsteak."

Mr. Jerome turned his horse. "We'll come back later for these wolves. Dwight, this bounty, added to the money you got for those other two, will send you to college. It's been a bad winter, but it's over, and we're all richer in more ways than one."

Dwight pulled Limpy back so he could ride beside Joe as they cantered down the slope toward the house.

"Are you really going to college, Dwight?" Joe asked.

"I haven't thought much about it, but Dad and Mom want me to."

"I wish I could," Joe said wistfully. "The big-league scouts get a lot of material from the college teams."

"Two for you, and two for me," said Dwight. "You kept me from shooting Lead, once. You stuck with me when no one else would. These two wolves belong to you. Dad's fair. He'll see it my way. And here we are home."

A huge, shaggy dog came out of the sheepshed and roared a fierce challenge as they approached the corral. His weight and sleekness and power showed what good care and good food had done for him. He had been ready to meet his wolves when at last the chance came.

Lead followed the two strange horses menacingly, until they had passed through the last gate. Dwight got off to examine the dog. Lead kept his eye on Bucky and Joe, growling softly, as Dwight's hands slipped over him, feeling for wounds.

"He's not hurt much. He whipped two wolves and came back to his sheep with scarcely a scratch. Now what do you think?"

Bucky said nothing.

In the sheepshed, a lamb became separated from its mother. It set up a sudden startled bleating. The big dog turned, still growling in his throat, and trotted back to see what was the matter. The bleating stopped. The huge dog lay down.

"How about it, Bucky, do you want him chained?" Mr. Jerome asked.

Bucky thought it over. "Let him run, Clay," he said. "There may be other wolves."

The back door of the house was flung open, and the three little girls came running to meet them. Trinket fell headlong. She got up crying, covered with snow. Mr. Jerome got off his horse and helped her up.

"Mamma said I could tell!" she wailed.

Mr. Jerome brushed the snow from her. "Tell what, honey?"

"Colleen's got some puppies in the coalpit."

"And she won't let anyone in," Christine cried.

"Please, Dwight, show them to us," Irene begged.

Colleen stood guard at the coalpit door, barring their way. Dwight took her by the collar, speaking sharply, and walked down the steps that had been cut into the lignite, the hound beside him. She was three years old and motherhood was new to her, and she did not even want Dwight bothering those squirming, squeaking things.

In a moment she seemed to realize that he meant no harm to her babies. She stopped growling. Her tail thumped the nest proudly.

"You can come down now, Dad," Dwight called. "Bring a lantern with you. She's all right as long as I'm here."

They came down slowly. Colleen's wild instinct had come back again, when she needed it. The lantern showed a neat nest of stolen feed sacks, shredded cornstalks, and old paper. In the midst of it were six tiny, squirming mites. Colleen's teeth flashed as Bucky touched one of them with his finger. Bucky jerked his hand back and Dwight caught the dog just in time.

"That one's the spitting image of the big mutt," said Bucky. "Dwight, how much will you take for that pup when he's weaned?"

"Why, Bucky, you never owned a dog in your life," said Mr. Jerome, smiling.

"That was last year," said Bucky. "Clay, a good wolf-killing dog strain can be the salvation of this country. I'll give you fifty dollars for that pup."

Mr. Jerome winked at his son, and Dwight suddenly found it hard to talk. When Bucky wanted one of his dogs—well, that was something!

"I don't think Dwight wants your money, Bucky," said Mr. Jerome. "The pup's yours."

"I hate to take him that way." Bucky squinted at Dwight. He grinned. "That's not all freckles that makes your face look so dirty, boy. Tell you what. I've got a brand-new razor I'm not using, and it's time you had one of your own. I'll swap you that razor for your pup."

"Aw—!" Dwight rubbed his cheeks in confusion. They *were* kind of bristly, at that. He'd been too busy this winter to keep track of such matters. "Well, all right, Bucky—if you insist," he said.